The Dark Islands Chronicles

The Prophecy Part One

C. J. Cole
&
J. Blackadder

Chapter I
How The
Mighty Have Fallen

From the shadows of the forest emerged a distorted figure, his face hidden by the worn, tattered dun coloured cloak that hung from his body. A scarred hand tightly gripped an aged knotted oak staff providing much needed support for his large frame. He staggered toward the edge of the woodland, hungry and exhausted. The other hand was hidden within the cloak, grasping the handle of his sword. These days it rarely left his firm grip. The man's breathing was ragged and laboured and his gaunt eyes winced as he passed from the dank darkness of the forest to the brightness beyond. He released the staff to raise his hand to shield his sensitive eyes. The sun's rays bathed him with light for the first time in almost a month. Searching longingly into the distance he strained yet further to see the outline of a small settlement through stinging eyes. *I am home,* he thought.

He removed his hood to reveal a weather worn face; his well-defined features masked by a course unkempt beard and framed by matted light brown hair that almost touched his shoulders. As his hazel eyes became more adjusted to the light, he could make out the settlement more clearly. It was almost exactly how he remembered it. Not a day had gone by since he left when he had not yearned to be with his family. It was the memory of this place, of Romney, that had seen him through the more testing periods of his life. Romney had kept him going, even when he was fighting on some distant battlefield surrounded by the acrid stench of death and decay.

Situated within a large estuary, Romney was a small port and fishing village that had evolved after the Romans began draining the surrounding marshland. Romney sat within the kingdom of Kent; whose coastline watched over the narrow stretch of water that separated the islands of Britain from mainland Europe.

These are the mysterious Romney Marshes, a small group of inter-tidal islands and sand-banks, separated by a network of creeks and small rivers that were fed from the sea.

The autumn breeze whipped across the open fields. It rustled the newly fallen leaves from the forest behind him, as it so often did on the exposed marsh. The sense of familiarity this invoked within him made him feel, at least for that moment, as though he had never left. He paused, listening intently, as the sound of children playing rang through the salty air, accompanied by the soothing melody of the sea gently lapping against the sandy shore.

The farms were alive, as the business of tending to the thousands of sheep that grazed upon the lush green fields was addressed. The harbour, busy with ships of all sizes, was bustling with life as cargoes were loaded, unloaded and haggled over on the quayside. Romney was a harbour predominantly of wool, conveniently produced by the sheep abundant on the Marsh and highly prized throughout Britain and Europe.

He crouched awkwardly to retrieve his staff that had fallen to the ground and, taking a moment to touch the soil he had known so well, he rubbed the rich soil between his heavily calloused fingers. After a moment or two he stood up, pulling his hood further over his face and continued onwards, his heart filling with an anxious joy at the thought of coming home. It was a joy mixed with apprehension and of curiosity. What changes had occurred during his prolonged absence?

Suddenly the order and familiarity that had enveloped the settlement was shattered by a piercing wail. The weary figure stopped in his tracks. He stood breathless as twelve huge black steeds with eyes of fire appeared on the outskirts of the settlement. The steeds were sweating and lathering as though they had been riding upon the wind. On their backs rode the most fearful of creatures, clad in heavy, slightly rusted black armour from stirrup to helmet.

The weary traveller had seen their ilk many times before and had witnessed the product of their despicable intentions. As he attempted to focus on the terrifying sight, the group of hellish raiders descended upon the settlement with spiteful intent. The village was thrown into pandemonium as the mysterious assailants began to set light to the buildings and hack indiscriminately at the villagers as they attempted to flee. Any lingering feelings he had of weariness and hunger fled his mind as he drew his long sword. The handle rarely left his grasp since it was placed back in its scabbard. He had long anticipated the return of these iron clad marauders – Dark Warriors – the remnants of an evil force others thought had been destroyed. He had known better. He wished his instinct had been wrong.

Discarding the tattered cloak into a crumpled heap and dropping the staff once more, he revealed the tunic that he had kept carefully hidden for so long. Upon it was the symbol of his Order, a red cross with a sword standing upright at its centre. This man was the last of the fifteen knights, remnants of the Brotherhood of the Sword. He was Asgrim of Romney. With his heart pounding and adrenaline coursing through him, he charged headlong into the midst of the chaos.

The villagers were defending themselves with anything they could lay their hands on. Their farm implements and staves were no match for the mounted assassins.

'Alwin!' cried Asgrim. Alwin spun around to see a warrior thundering towards him. He attempted to cut the horse down with a scythe but was rendered unconscious, falling, before he could use his weapon. The Warrior unsheathed its sword and was poised to strike a fatal blow when, suddenly, instantly aware of Asgrim within their midst, the Dark Warriors attention was drawn to the knight.

‘We’ve been expecting you!’ a Warrior, its voice raspy and serpent-like, called.

Asgrim readjusted his sword for a firmer grip in both hands and stood his ground. ‘I will not let you harm these people!’ he hollered defiantly. The thought that these were his people fuelling his resolve.

Casting about him, the knight found himself encircled by the other horsemen. It had been over a decade since he had last confronted this many of them. He tried not to think of what lay beneath the armour. These terrible creatures were vile; half living, half corpse, they were the decaying remnants of men. The product of unholy sorcery, yet despite their putrefying flesh they were strong and protected by jagged armour that induced fear into the heart of even the bravest of soldiers. Their hate-filled and unnatural yellow eyes blazed through two slits in their helmets; a hideous indication of the malignant presence lurking within the dim interior of each iron shell.

Aware that there would be no quarter given, Asgrim had at least afforded the villagers a chance to escape. He knew it was *him* the warriors had been seeking.

'You can do nothing! You are the last of your Order!' snarled another of the creatures, pointing accusingly at the knight.

Asgrim turned; 'That's as may be, but I'll go down fighting!' he roared, glancing around at the beasts that encompassed him. Calmly, he approached the warrior that had taunted him, his anger and hatred welling up inside him with every step. Asgrim may have grown older since his last encounter with these sordid miscreants, but his resolve was still solid and his reflexes just as sharp as ever. Before any of the Warriors could react, he swiftly swung his sword with all his accumulated strength. The blade tore through the filthy beast's arm, severing it at the elbow. The dead limb smouldered foully in its iron tomb as it hit the ground. Whilst the creature screamed in pain, cradling the torn flesh and shattered bone, Asgrim raised his sword again and brought it crashing down into the Warrior's armour with such ferocity that he was showered in sparks as the metal split in two. The steel plunged into the Warrior's chest, piercing the void where there once was a human heart. It's place now a reservoir of hatred and bile, for there was no room for a heart in this creature. Any semblance of compassion or tenderness, anything that could reveal this had once been a man, was long gone.

The Warrior fell from his horse and landed like a pile of scrap, the iron clattering as it hit the ground, thick black blood seeping from the broken armour. Asgrim retrieved his sword with a sickly suck and was poised, ready to strike another warrior. As he turned, he was brought to his knees by a tremendous blow to the back of his head, It had arrived without warning and was swiftly followed by another blow, then another, and yet another. The Warriors continued to beat him until he was barely conscious, sufficiently aware to feel pain but unable to mount any form of defence.

'Your God cannot protect you now!' cried one of the horsemen, raising its visor to spit upon the twisted form of the knight, 'but you can die like him!' its voice filled with contempt and eager anticipation of what was to come.

The Warriors dismounted their steeds and dragged Asgrim's broken body to the entrance of a nearby barn. Two thrust him against the door, lifted him off the ground and rendered him dangling and helpless whilst the others drew their daggers. Asgrim writhed and roared in agony as the blades tore through his flesh, first one wrist and then the other pinning him to the door like an insect. Unable to speak, Asgrim could only look on in horror as one of the warriors knelt before him, his dagger unsheathed. The evil beast looked him up and down. Fortunately for Asgrim, he could not see its sadistic smile hidden beneath the vicious armour.

There was a terrible sound of bones breaking like dried twigs underfoot as the weapon tore into Asgrim's shins, impaling both of his legs to the tough wood of the barn door. The knight screamed inwardly but not a sound from him was heard. Searing pain shot through his entire body filling him with unbearable agony. As they were walking away, one of the warriors noticed Asgrim's fallen sword lying on the ground nearby. The creature picked it up, raised the blade above its head and ran at speed towards his defenceless victim. Asgrim's terror-filled eyes opened wide and he tried ripping his wrists from the blades that suspended him. They were driven in too deep and there was to be no escape. The warrior's armour was spattered with blood as the sword was rammed hard through Asgrim's chest, through the other side of his carcass and straight through the wooden door. He drove the blade home right to the hilt. The terrible sound of Asgrim's spine shattering crunched in his ears as the blade was twisted to ensure there was no chance of the wound healing. His blood gargled in his throat and was expelled in large gouts as, once again, he tried to scream. As if in a final insult, the horses let out the most fearful snarl, gloating at the man that dangled broken before them. Content that they had fulfilled their master's wicked bidding, they rode away across the Marsh leaving the knight and the remnants of the ravaged village in their wake.

It was daybreak before true extent of the damage to the smouldering homesteads became clear and the remaining villagers, who had fled to the nearby forests, for safety cautiously returned and began to survey the ruins of their homes. There was little that had escaped unscathed, most dwellings were raised to the ground or ravaged beyond saving. Pockets of fire were still visible and the stench of charred remains hung heavy in the morning mist, mingling with the pall of lingering smoke.

Alwin returned to his farmhouse only to discover that it had been completely destroyed. He had lived in the settlement at Romney for his entire life. His wife,

Eugenia, moved to Britain from Osnabruck, Lower Saxony, when she was fifteen. Three years later she and Alwin had been married in the small chapel in the centre of Romney. She had died seven years ago, having perished during the birth of their youngest daughter, Elspeth, leaving Alwin to manage the farmstead and bring up their three children alone.

Alwin began the frantic search for his children, having gotten separated from them just before their farmhouse was torched. He could not find any trace of any of them. The search took on a new urgency as he wandered amongst the charred and bloodied bodies of his friends and neighbours that had been hacked down indiscriminately. These were people he had known for years. He searched through the debris of shattered buildings and under piles of rubble that had once been the village he had known all his life. He searched through all the detritus that was scattered all about but still could find no sign of them. On the edge of the village was a structure that was still gently alight but had miraculously remained standing. As he looked up through the flames of what once had been a cattle shed, he could see the faint silhouettes of figures in the gloom. 'Freyja, Elspeth, Falhinir?' he shouted, but he could not hear any answer. As he rushed toward the shed, he could make out the shape of others too and realised that most of the surviving villagers, including his own beloved brood had gathered at the entrance to the barn. The only structure that had remained intact.

The sight that greeted him when he reached the barn filled him with horror and utter shock, his stomach lurched and his blood ran cold as he laid his eyes upon the crucified knight. Bile rose in his throat and he fought the sudden urge to throw up. He cautiously approached the inert and defiled body of Asgrim as the villagers looked on in silence.

'Help me get him down, Falhinir!' exclaimed Alwin.

The sixteen-year-old could not tear

his terrified eyes away from Asgrim's scarred and bloodied face as he stepped towards the mutilated knight. Blood flowed in a steady torrent from the broken body as he and his father removed the daggers from his wrists and shins and discarded them. Both Falhinir and his father struggled between them to remove the knight's great sword from where it was wedged so tightly in his chest.

Alwin's huge six-foot frame took the weight of the broken man as they released him and laid him gently upon the ground. Falhinir felt his stomach froth and could taste vomit in the back of his throat as his feet were sucked into the earth that had become sodden with Asgrim's blood. He knew that to be sick now would be a disgrace to both himself, his family and to the brave knight who lay before him so he used every fibre of his being to fight down his feelings of nausea and ensure the contents of his stomach remained where they were.

Suddenly Asgrim let out a huge gasp,

terrifying all those who had gathered round who had assumed him dead.

'He's still alive, we will need some help getting him inside,' Alwin gasped looking at the other villagers. Three stout men who had extinguished the small fires in the barn whilst the body was cut down, helped carry the broken knight inside. They laid him down in some straw that still carpeted the hard ground. Some of the more suggestible villagers began to mutter under their breath of religion and of Christ as they saw the crucifix shaped blood stain soaked into the barn door. A few even ran in the direction of what had once been the church before realising the futility of the gesture and returning, not wanting to miss what was going on in the barn.

'Freyja, fetch a bowl of water, mugwort, wolfsbane, sage and some cloth,' ordered Alwin with a shaken voice.

Falhinir was kneeling beside the knight, when a cold and bloodstained hand suddenly reached up and grabbed him. He let out a terrified gasp.

'Try not to move, Asgrim,' said Alwin as he rested his hand on the knight's arm.

Falhinir looked at his father in astonishment. 'How do you know his name?" he asked. His father did not answer him as he continued to tie pieces of cloth tightly around the wounds on Asgrim's wrists.

'Alwin, is it really you?' Asgrim gurgled, his voice distorted by the wounds round his mouth and the blood that had pooled in his throat.

'Yes, old friend,' Alwin replied as Asgrim's eyes filled with tears, 'you finally made it home." "Look after him, Falhinir,' he continued, 'keep pressure on his chest wound and I will be back in a short while.' Alwin got up and went outside to look for Freyja.

Falhinir failed to acknowledge his father as his gaze was fixed on Asgrim's atrocious wounds and was barely able to speak. It was he that had discovered Asgrim on the door, the image burned into his memory, tormenting him.

‘There isn’t much time,’ Asgrim sighed. He looked at the young boy at his side. ‘You must be Falhinir.’

‘You know my name?’ Falhinir replied, ‘try not to move,’ he continued after a short pause, barely able to recognise the distorted and shattered face as a human being.

Asgrim took a deep gargled breath. ‘I am your mother’s brother. You are too young to remember when I left to fight,’ he said feebly whilst choking and accidentally spattering his nephew with blood. Falhinir fell back in both horror and disgust. ‘Fight who? Who did this to you, and us, why?’ he asked as he tore off a piece of Asgrim’s tunic to clean both himself and his uncle. Asgrim tightened his grip on Falhinir’s arm, the blood from his wrist leaking through the bandage. ‘Tuan, an evil Sorcerer. He must be stopped. You are the last in the bloodline. It is your responsibility now, Falhinir. You must go. Become a knight of the Brotherhood. Fulfil the prophecy.’ Falhinir wiped away a thick trickle of blood that was running from Asgrim's lips, mostly to ensure that he was not spattered again. 'Go to the cliffs... Dover,' the knight continued, now barely able to talk, 'there... you... receive assistance from Hengest and... Horsa. They hold the information... find the Book.' Falhinir looked at his uncle with a vacant stare. 'What Prophecy? What book? I don't understand.' With a shaking hand Asgrim pulled a blood-stained parchment from the depths of his tunic. Falhinir hesitantly took the document and with that his uncle's grasp loosened and he breathed no more.

Alwin and Freyja returned with the water and a cloth. Alwin knelt beside Asgrim's body. 'Hold still Asgrim. Asgrim?'

'He's gone,' said Falhinir with an unsteady tremble in his voice. Alwin placed his palm on Asgrim's bloody forehead. 'Welcome home Asgrim,' he uttered under his breath, fighting to hold back his tears.

A cold wind swept across the marsh as the sun rose over Romney. Falhinir looked out to sea towards Dover, the sword blade of the Brotherhood hanging from his waist. Asgrim's final words had been playing on his mind for the last two nights. He still felt resentment toward his uncle for leading the warriors to his home but he was intrigued. Asgrim had told him that he had to embark upon some mysterious quest. What he had heard had sounded like the ramblings of a deranged man. The knight had sustained serious injuries that might have affected his reasoning. Maybe there was no book, no quest, no Brotherhood and certainly no evil sorcerer. It sounded exciting and more than a little dangerous and he was slightly apprehensive as he considered what he should do. When he actually thought about it, he realised that as much as he enjoyed living in Romney, he had never really travelled far from home and he had certainly never left Kent. It was only a relatively short trip to Dover and on a clear day he could see the white cliffs from the Marsh, if it turned out there was nothing in Asgrim's words then at least he did not have far to go. He'd be back before anyone noticed and it certainly wasn't anything that he needed to trouble his father or his siblings over. Nothing to discuss really, he'd just go to Dover and have a scout around and be back before he was missed. Still contemplating what his uncle had said, he drew the great sword from its scabbard. To his surprise it was light and easy to handle. Carefully, he inspected the blade and as he did so the sunlight glistened on the metal. Falhinir had never seen such a weapon as this before. He had seen many swords but none so grand as that which he held in his palm. This was a weapon made of steel and beautifully crafted, unlike the dull iron blades produced by the village blacksmith. The hilt was solid bronze and sat comfortably against his clenched fist. The leather-bound handle was soft and seemed to mould to the shape of his fingers. The end of the handle was fashioned into a mounted crest, and in it was inscribed the distinctive cross and sword emblem of what he imagined to be, The Brotherhood of the

Sword. Falhinir ran his fingers over the tempered steel and found it cool against his skin. He noticed a small trickle of blood seeping from his forefinger, yet he felt no pain. The blade must be very sharp indeed thought Falhinir. Suddenly a strange sense of calm washed over him and he felt different somehow, as if the blade had connected with him in some small way. He didn't know why, but in that one defining moment it was as though everything became clear to him. What his uncle said was true. He knew, in that moment, that he would have no choice but to embark upon this quest, to fulfil the prophecy. Placing the sword back in its scabbard, he squeezed a little more blood from the small wound and looked into the sky. As he gazed into the clear blue distance, he swore a blood oath that he would honour his uncle's wishes and avenge his murder as though he were talking to Asgrim's ghost itself.

Later that day the villagers gathered in the graveyard of St. Lawrence's, their small timber church had perished but, hey, they would rebuild, in time. The ground was still sacred as they came together to pay their final respects and honour the brave knight whose sacrifice had ensured their survival. Alwin and Falhinir placed Asgrim's body into the cold sandy soil in a grave cut beside his sister, Eugenie, Alwin' wife. A tear fell from Falhinir's eye as the ground received the body of his uncle. His father had told him stories about his uncle the previous evening, of the adventures he'd had and why he decided to became a Knight of the Brotherhood of the Sword. He told of how Asgrim had embarked on his calling, following an encounter with a member of the Order, who was staying at the local inn. He had been regaled with tales of the knight's own adventures and it had fired in Asgrim an ambition to serve God and protect his faith. Falhinir wished he had gotten to know his uncle, but he knew in his heart that Asgrim was a brave and noble man and for now, he felt that was enough.

Freyja and Elspeth clutched their

father's hands as the two monks who had lived in the church said prayers for Asgrim. They had never seen or heard of this great man before, yet they somehow felt his death represented a great loss for them.

Falhinir had still not yet told his father what Asgrim had said to him. He wondered if was really ought to explain to him that he must leave and follow the path that had been presented to him. The day passed very slowly as Falhinir pondered his predicament.

Forced to sleep in a rundown stable, Alwin put his daughters to bed and walked into an adjacent room where Falhinir was waiting for him. 'I need to tell you something father,' Falhinir started nervously.

'What is it son?' asked Alwin.

Falhinir looked at his father pensively. 'Before he died, uncle told me of why he had been away. He told me that he had been fighting a war against an evil Sorcerer.'

'Yes, I know,' answered Alwin, his eyes

staring vacantly at the fire which burned brightly in the centre of the room, he knew where this conversation was leading. 'I also know that you have been passed a great responsibility,' he continued.

A puzzled look came over Falhinir's face. 'How did you know that?'

Alwin felt a pang of raw emotion stab his heart. He wanted to lie to his son but he could not. 'The truth is; I overheard Asgrim talking to you whilst I was waiting for Freyja to return with the water. Son, you are sixteen, and almost a man. I am not going to try and stop you from leaving. If your uncle is right, then you are the only one who can end the wars and stop all the senseless deaths.' Alwin placed his hands on his son's shoulders. 'I do not want you to leave us, but I know that you will not fail in your task ahead and that you will make me proud, your sisters proud, your mother proud and your uncle proud.' This was a profound speech from Alwin, who was a man of few words and the impact of such utterances was not lost on Falhinir.

'I will father, I promise,' Falhinir replied, 'I do not know when I will return, but I hope it will not be so long.'

Falhinir walked silently into the room where his sisters were sleeping and kissed them each gently on their foreheads. Picking up his few belongings, he and Alwin walked to the door. Falhinir hugged his father one last time, feeling a surge of both excitement and sadness. He turned and walked away, silently passing Asgrim's grave. It was as though he was being sure not to wake him from his slumber as he faded into the darkness of the Romney Marshes.

Chapter II

Hengest and Horsa

As the fierce waves ferociously crashed against the dark granite cliff face, the wind whistled its eerie tune through the caves of the Lizard Peninsula. This is a place where few will tread. It is a place from which people seldom return. Those who dared are rarely heard from again for Tuan and his evil Dark Warriors inhabit these lands.

From within the darkness of his lair, Tuan could see the eleven shadowy figures entering the cave through the ethereal mist that constantly shrouds the peninsula. These were his Dark Warriors. His obedient soldiers, willing to execute any sadistic task Tuan asked of them. They lit their torches and cautiously but defiantly approached their master.

The dim silhouette of their master stirred, casting a long shadow upon the wall of the cave and accentuated by the flickering torchlight. Tuan rarely ventured into the light, for to him it was a painful reminder of everything that was once good in the world, a time when he lived in peace with his family and their tribe, before the dark times, before death and destruction ravaged his homelands.

Despite being halfway into his regeneration, he was still very weak. His hair had grown long and was white, as was his beard, obscuring his wizened features. His long, once bright robes, bearing various icons of his Pagan beliefs, were shabby and worn, and the numerous items of jewellery and trinkets that festooned his sparse frame were faded and dirty. It was all he could do to sit and meditate and his powers of witchcraft were lamentably feeble.

Tuan restlessly fiddled with the cracked and discoloured amethyst beads that clung to the skeletal wrist of his right hand as his Warriors approached him.

'It is done Master,' proudly boasted one of the beasts. 'The Order is no more.'

Tuan's booming voice resounded from the darkness. At least he still sounded strong and vibrant he thought. 'What of their families, are they dead too?'

'We are sure they are all dead,' a Warrior replied with glee.

Tuan erupted with fury. 'They are not all dead!' he exclaimed, feeling nothing but contempt towards his now terrified minions. These wretched souls meant nothing to him, just a means to an end. The Warriors cowered, simultaneously shielding themselves from pieces of rubble that fell as Tuan's voice echoed through the cave. Tuan rose and approached his Warriors, at over six-foot-four inches in height, he towered over them. 'The fault is probably mine', said Tuan, as he removed one Warrior's helmet, revealing the tormented creature within. 'I did this to you in the hope that you would obey my every command. Clearly not all of you understand this.' Tuan placed his hands upon the creature's head. 'Perhaps I should help you to understand!' His face became contorted with hate filled rage as he crushed the Warrior's skull between his bare hands. The bone shattered, spilling what little contents there were on the floor of the cave. 'I hope this little lesson has clarified your position here' he said, squeezing brain matter through his fingers. The other Warriors watched in horror as the lifeless body fell to the floor, each one desperately hoping they wouldn't be next. Tuan took a deep sighing breath. 'There is a boy,' he said calmly, clutching at the ancient golden beryl scrying pendant that hung from his neck. This was the source of his ability to look out from beyond his domain, and witness events as they occur. 'This boy has the blood of the Brotherhood running through his veins, and he knows of the book. He must not be allowed to find the location of Ceridwen. For centuries the cruel bastards of this land have raped and plundered my home,' he said solemnly. In a rare lapse of concentration, he cast his mind back to the day that changed his life forever; the day *they* came from the sea, *the Britons*:

The island of Eire, 28 B.C.: 'Tuan! Tuan!' cried the young woman, 'look, ships!' Tuan ran to the edge of the fort that overlooked the sea. 'They are not ours,' he said staring into the distance. 'We must prepare for attack! Ǽloch, my love, you and the other women! take the children away from here! Quickly! As fast as you can to the tall woodlands and seek shelter with the Elders, they will protect you.' The Elders were the sages of their tribe who had for centuries retreated to natural groves within the heavily forested areas, leaving the more open spaces of their tribe's lands to younger and more fruitful heirs. Their surroundings brought them closer to nature and the Gods they worshipped and consulted. However, now was not the time to be seeking their advice or wisdom but their help and defence against the approaching invaders.

The Britons spilled from their boats, letting forth their battle cry as they laid siege to the huge ring fort. Tuan and his people had constructed their defences with their bare hands in preparation for this day. Consisting of four ditches and ramparts in concentric rings, this was one of the largest forts of its kind in Eire and could be clearly seen for miles around. This attack was revenge for a failed attempt several months ago. On that day, many of the Briton's had perished but Tuan's homeland had remained steadfast.

Tuan's men stood firm atop the fort, their bows and arrows, slings and iron spears trained on their targets, whilst others nervously clutched swords and shields. The air was surprisingly still and gave no indication of the impending battle. That soon changed on the order to repel. Tuan's soldiers met the invaders with a wall of angry shouting and whooping. Neither side could understand what the other was yelling but the meaning was clear as the invaders began to ascend the enormous ramparts. The Irish replied with a hail of rocks, spears and arrows. Tuan and his men cheered as the Britons fell, but soon several had managed to scale the ramparts. Tuan's men found themselves engaged in close-quarters fighting, clearly outmatched by the Briton's superior weaponry and fine iron swords. The acrid stench of hatred filled sweat filled the air mixed with the flinty tang of the blood of countless men as it seeped into the earth.

After three hours of relentless bloodshed, the fighting was done. Tuan and his warriors had stood their ground bravely but they were no match for the rampaging Britons, who had outnumbered the Irish four-to-one. Only a small number of Tuan's tribe endured. A few souls had attempted to escape the fort and reach the sanctuary of the woodlands. They were soon captured having, unwittingly, led the Britons to the refuge of the women, children and Elders.

Tuan looked on helplessly as his remaining tribes folk were shackled and paraded like animals back to the fort. The Britons showed no mercy as they taunted and decapitated them one by one, before taking their severed heads as trophies. Tears of inconsolable sorrow stung his eyes and hatred and rage parched this throat as his heavily pregnant wife was systematically and repeatedly raped before him. Ǽloch cried out for mercy as swords were driven into her swollen belly, killing the unborn child within. Tuan tried to struggle free as the leader of the invading Britons, a man they called Vilux, stood over the almost lifeless body of his wife. Tuan felt a pain like no other as he saw his still twitching son ripped from his mother's womb. Ǽloch writhed uncontrollably until a violent blow from an axe tore through her delicate neck, bringing with it a swift end to her torment. Tuan wept but could muster no more tears as his wife's head was carried away by her long brown hair, her eyes fixed ahead with a vacant, gaze. Vilux ordered the execution of Tuan and the removal of his head as he and the rest of his men swaggered back to the shore carrying their grizzly prizes with them. One more head to add to the pile already awaiting them in the footwells of their boats.

Tuan was held upright, his head tilted back and his throat exposed. He could feel the cold metal of a blade against his skin, but he did not care; he was immune to any further suffering and was ready to embrace his release. A sudden outburst of shouting occurred to his left and his would-be executioner collapsed like a rotten log. He was dead, two arrows protruding from his neck. Anticipating an ambush, the remainder of the Britons fled to the beaches and into their vessels. Tuan recognised his rescuers as men from a neighbouring tribe and although they had not always lived in harmony, they were united by their loathing of the Britons. One of the Elders had evaded capture and managed to alert the nearby settlement. They freed Tuan, who swore eternal revenge upon all the Britons. He denounced all peaceful traditions of his culture, as taught him by the Elders and embraced the more sinister aspects of his Celtic religion. Tuan abandoned his home and tribe, to live like an animal in the forest. It was here where he felt closer to his new found gods, Morrigan, Queen of the Underworld and Donn, Lord of the Dead. His new companions offered to reveal to him the secrets of eternal life in return for the souls of any poor unfortunates that may stray among the dark avenues of the forests.

Tuan revelled in his new found savagery, murdering scores of innocents, learning more of the sinister secrets of immortality with every life he stole. Morrigan anointed him with the blood of children and bestowed upon him her pendant, so that he may use to achieve his ultimate ambition - to destroy the Britons and live forever.

The distant screams of the past brought Tuan back to the present. He once again clutched the pendant and took a deep breath. 'The boy is travelling to the white caves in the Eastern cliffs. Do not let him leave them alive. Now, go!'

The Warriors slunk from their

master's presence to embark upon their murderous journey. The sound of their horses' hooves rumbled into the distance as they thundered through the sea mists and across the open lands of the Dumnonian kingdom to the Eastern Cliffs and the boy who was making his way there.

Tuan, about to return to his meditation, suddenly became aware of a presence. The old sorcerer's black, soulless eyes pierced the darkness and from the shadows stepped a black shrouded figure. 'I can get close to the boy,' uttered a grainy voice from within the black cloak, 'If he does find Ceridwen, you will have the book. Nothing will stop you then and you will have wreaked your revenge and unleashed your wrath upon the people of these lands.'

'Very well,' answered Tuan, 'but if you should fail me...'

'I won't,' interrupted the voice from the darkness, 'and remember you do not have the power to fully control me.' Wrapping his cloak tightly around him, he retreated from the cave, leaving Tuan to continue his meditation.

Falhinir looked out across the sea as the sun rose over the horizon. He opened his small leather bag and ate a little of the bread and cheese he had packed the night before. As he cast around to determine his location in relation to the map, he carried he noticed the rise of the cliffs in the distance. He was almost at his destination. Packing up his meagre breakfast, he pressed onward. Within couple of hours Falhinir found himself standing above the white chalky cliffs of Dover, now all he had to do was locate the caves of Hengest and Horsa.

This is not going to be easy! Falhinir thought to himself. Peering down over the edge of the steep cliff face, he could vaguely identify a rough path leading down to the base of the cliff. Falhinir found the chalk was loose beneath his feet as he set about his dangerous descent; his hands were soon white and his fingertips bleeding from desperately grasping onto anything that would result in him not plummeting to his death. Falhinir paused for a moment, perching himself upon a small outcrop, to catch his breath. As he attempted to bring his breathing under control, he became aware of a faint voice emanating from one of the many caves that pock marked the cliff face. As he craned his neck and searched around in an attempt to pinpoint the sound, Falhinir suddenly felt slightly giddy and somewhat nauseated. It was a peculiar feeling and one he had never experienced before Having spent his entire life up until that point among the level fields of Romney Marsh, this was the highest above the ground he had ever been. Even though the marshes were flanked by a range of hills, he had never ventured this far from home before. Falhinir cast his mind back to the many times he had helped his father thatch the roof of the house, remembering that he thought he was pretty high up. It was nothing compared to the sound of the waves of the English Channel dramatically thundering into Dover's white cliffs. The noise brought him back to the present, along with the urgent desire to get off the cliff as soon as possible. He fought down any residual feelings of vertigo and pushed his back against the wall of the cliff. The clumsy movement loosened the chalk beneath his feet and suddenly, without warning, he found himself slipping uncontrollably towards the edge of his perch. He stretched out his arms and desperately began clawing at the chalk. It was not sufficient, he could find no purchase as he fell, arms flailing and clutching at air, over the edge of the cliff towards the treacherous boulders strewn about the shoreline below.

With his eyes tightly screwed he tumbled downward, letting out an anguished yell as he smashed his right arm and whacked his head on landing. Falhinir dare not move for a moment, fearing the worst. Cautiously he opened his eyes and looking up he could see that he only dropped a short distance. He was in fact, sprawled in front of a cave completely invisible from above. Getting to his feet, he checked himself over and winced as he felt a small cut to the side of his forehead. He had got off extremely lightly and once he had made sure he was still in possession of all of his belongings, he brushed himself off and surveyed the mouth of the cave for any signs of habitation. There appeared to be none, however, the prospect of venturing deeper into the cave did not appeal to him much either. As he was half way down the cliff and there was definitely no way down he had little choice but to travel further into the cave. He stared with a degree of trepidation into the darkness for he did not know what was waiting for him. Gingerly he trod deeper into the clammy cave, his eyes flitting about him furiously as anxiety increased with every step. Centuries of weathering had scoured the cave's interior, producing unusual rock formations that developed a sinister appearance in the perpetual gloom. Thick layers of moss lined the chalk walls, giving the formations personal features. Falhinir's heart began to race as the daylight slowly ebbed away with each delicate step that took him further from the cave entrance. Then, as he moved into the shadow of a large boulder, he thought he could see a light flickering towards the back wall of the cave. He had no idea how far inside the cliff he had travelled but he knew it must have been some distance from the sea because the air was now dry and the moss had given way to bare rock. The truth was he had walked almost a quarter of a mile inland. The soft chalk having been washed away with millennia of relentless rain and wind. Peering around the large rock he could see the faint outline of a person sitting beside a large crackling fire. Falhinir's blood was pounding in his ears as he called out nervously to the mysterious figure.

'Hello?'

The person jumped to their feet. 'What the... Who's there, who are you, what do you want? Get out of my cave!'

Falhinir stepped out from behind the boulder. He could see the figure more clearly now, and to his astonishment he found the mysterious figure to be that of a short, stout old man. More than sixty years in age and no more than five feet in height, his hair was cropped and greying with a slightly reddish tint. His aged features were masked by a short stubbly beard. His clothes, patched and shabby, had obviously seen many a years' service.

Falhinir cautiously approached the strange hermit. 'My name is Falhinir of Romney, and I have come in search of Hengest and Horsa.'

The small man marched up to Falhinir, sticking his chest out. 'They are not here! So, go away!'

'Do you know where I may find them?' enquired Falhinir, ignoring the man's rude behaviour and bad manners.

'No, I told you, I don't know", he repeated slowly, enunciating every word, implying Falhinir may have not been all that intelligent, 'besides, they are dead you bloody fool!'

Falhinir pleaded again with the ageing stranger. 'I know this, and I know that I may sound out of my mind, but I need to find them. Please, if you know of anything that may help me find them, please tell me.'

'Why do you seek them?' asked the old man.

'I am,' Falhinir hesitated for a brief moment, 'I am on a quest,' he continued cautiously, not wanting to give the strange fellow too much information about his reasons for intruding and not wanting to invade the old man's privacy. 'I have been sent upon an important quest by my uncle to find the great Hengest and Horsa.'

'I see,' he replied suspiciously, 'and your uncle, know them well, did he?'

'Of course he didn't!' Falhinir snapped in reply, knowing that the old man was being awkward. Hengest and Horsa had died over four centuries before his uncle was born, everyone knew that. 'My uncle was the last of the great fifteen knights of a sacred Order. He has sent me to find Hengest and Horsa so that an ancient prophecy may be fulfilled. I do not understand it either, but this is what I must do.' Falhinir sensed he was wasting his time. 'I am sorry for disturbing you.' Falhinir turned and slowly began to walk back towards the light that illuminated the entrance of the cave.

The old man's green eyes glistened as he stared at Falhinir's back and called out. 'The Brotherhood, the Order of which you speak, it is the Brotherhood of the Sword is it not?'

As Falhinir turned, the man sat down and began to stroke his unshaved chin.

'You've heard of them?' asked Falhinir walking back to the man and taking a seat at his side.

'Yes, I have heard of them!' he barked, and then something surprising happened. His hard features began to soften and his temper changed from that of agitation to what Falhinir thought was reminiscence or remorse even. 'I remember when the Order was as proud and strong as any army I had ever seen, we commanded thousands of brave men, but that was a long time ago, just memories now, they are, all gone, all dead.' He muttered darkly, looking at

Falhinir.

'You were one of the knights?' asked Falhinir with a look of disbelief. 'My uncle told me he was the last of the Order.

The old man looked up at the boy. 'Who was your uncle?'

'Asgrim of Romney,' Falhinir replied boldly.

'I remember him,' replied the stranger, gazing vacantly at the fire, 'he was perhaps the finest swordsman I had ever met.'

'And you were once a knight yourself?' Asked Falhinir, finding he was unable to believe that this scrawny little fellow was once part of one of the greatest Orders in Europe.

'Yes, I was once a knight just like your uncle, but with one exception.'

'What is that?'

'I trained the knights in the skills that they would need to command in battle.'

Falhinir could not believe his ears. The boy assumed that the man was either a fantasist or not quite right in his head. Falhinir felt anger swelling within him. It was one thing for this old codger to say he was a knight. But to even suggest that he had skills that surpassed those of his uncle, and that it was he that had actually mentored Asgrim well, that was quite preposterous. He leapt to his feet intent on giving this little man a piece of his mind, when a strange mist suddenly began to fill the cave. Falhinir looked on bewildered, for when it had cleared, he was confronted by two tall men. They were dressed in lavish furs, the attire reminiscent of Saxon royalty. Falhinir, totally taken aback, suddenly realised that it must be Hengest and Horsa that were standing before him. They did not look as he expected. When he embarked upon his journey to Dover, the thought of encountering ghosts upset him a little, but he found that his fears were misplaced. He did not experience any anxiety at all when confronted by the two ethereal brothers. In its place was awe. He was in awe of these two great men. He had grown up hearing of their deeds. These men, for they were men and quite solid, were legends personified.

'We have been watching you, Falhinir of Romney. This is my brother Horsa and I am...'

'Hengest,' Falhinir interjected.

'We know of your quest and we know that you seek the Book of Ceridwen.'

Falhinir stood in silence. He was finding it difficult to comprehend that he was in the company of the ghosts of two of the most accomplished Saxons in the history of his people.

Horsa turned to the old man. 'Sebastian, you will train this boy, and bestow upon him the knowledge of the Brotherhood.'

Sebastian looked at the spirit with a look of distain. 'Me, train this, this boy! Look at him, there's nothing of him!'

'Sebastian, you know what is at stake,' said Horsa firmly, 'Falhinir will need all the skills at our disposal if he is to defeat Tuan.'

'I'm tougher than you think old man!' Falhinir interjected angrily.

Sebastian looked at Falhinir sternly. 'Old

man is I indeed? I'll show you who the old man is!' Mumbling to himself, Sebastian strode off into the darkness.

'Where's he going?' Falhinir asked.

'To get his sword I wouldn't wonder,' replied Hengest with a hint of a grin.

'Sword!' exclaimed Falhinir looking a little alarmed.

'We won't let him harm you.' assured Hengest.

Sebastian re-emerged a short while later with a large iron broadsword in his practiced fist. Falhinir tried not to show his fear, given the fact that he had never used a sword before in his life. He stood his ground as Sebastian began to advance towards him. In truth, Sebastian was just as scared of Falhinir as Falhinir was of Sebastian especially as Sebastian was having a little difficulty carrying around the mighty weapon. It had been the best part of ten years since he had last used such a fearsome object and he was feeling a little rusty when confronted with the youthful stranger. 'I will show you what an old man can do!' Sebastian shouted. The idea of a strapping boy besting him in a fight in his own home, especially in front of Hengest and Horsa, enraged him a little. Falhinir unsheathed his sword and readied himself to take the first blow. Sebastian lifted the great sword above his head. Falhinir shut his eyes in anticipation when suddenly Sebastian let out a loud shriek followed by a dull thud. 'What the? Oh, bloody hell!'

Falhinir could hear Hengest and Horsa lauding heartily as he cautiously opened one eye. The broadsword had turned out to be a bit too heavy for the old man and as he lifted it above his head, it pulled him over backwards, sending him crashing to the ground and rolling off down towards the back of the cave, hitting the far wall. Falhinir ran down into the darkness where he found Sebastian on the ground cursing loudly and eloquently. It was enough to make the young man's ears go pink.

'Why don't we start from the beginning?' suggested Falhinir, helping Sebastian to his feet and cutting off the stream of curse words. 'Perhaps you're right,' replied Sebastian with a rueful grin.

Horsa and Hengest gave the pair a stern look. 'Enough of this, there is much to be done, if you are to defeat Tuan. We don't have much time; your training must begin immediately.'

For nigh on a month Sebastian trained Falhinir and taught him the ways of the Brotherhood of the Sword. Falhinir was schooled in the various skills needed in times of conflict. He was taught how to think, move and fight in hand-to-hand combat. Sebastian, a far better archer than a swordsman, tutored his young friend in the techniques of both the blade and the bow. Soon Falhinir had learnt the basics. Practice then honed the abilities he would come to rely on. Little did either of them realise how soon it would be before his new found talents would be tested against a real enemy.

Night had fallen over cliffs of Dover.

The autumn moon was full and bright as Falhinir sat in the mouth of the cave and looked out over the sea and across the bay towards his beloved Romney Marsh. The subtle turn of the seasons had brought with it great change for Falhinir. As he sat contemplating the events of the last few weeks, his thoughts turned to his family and the farm. Normally at this time of year the crops of the harvest would be stored, ready for the winter months. The dogs would be brought inside and his sisters would help tend to the sheep and ponies, whilst he and his father would move the pigs and cattle into the warmth of the barn, sheltering them from the frosts and chill winds. He wished he was there right now, but he already knew that things could never be the same again. Falhinir felt a shiver of loneliness as he realised it had been well over a month since he had last seen his family. He knew that they were physically not far away but it felt like a whole lifetime ago since he had seen them.

The night air was cold and still as

Falhinir's eyes drifted from the faint outline of the marsh coast to the oily darkness of the English Channel. Illuminated by the moon's benevolent rays, he watched the calm waves of the sea gently brush against the shore. He felt a sudden chill and without warning a general feeling of foreboding washed over him. Not knowing what this meant, he decided to find Sebastian and seek his advice.

Hengest and Horsa were waiting for Falhinir when he returned to the depths of the cave, while Sebastian had begun packing their few belongings into a large leather saddlebag. 'There have been developments,' said Hengest ominously, 'We believe Tuan knows that you are seeking the Book of Ceridwen, it is not safe for you to remain here.'

'How?' asked Falhinir.

'We cannot know for certain,' said Horsa stepping forward, 'but because of the events that occurred the last time the Brotherhood fought Tuan's forces, we have reason to believe he is still in possession of the Pendant of Morrigan.'

'What is the pendant of Morrigan?' Falhinir asked confused.

'The pendant is an ancient Pagan relic that once belonged to a powerful priestess called Morrigan; Queen of the Demons, who lived around a thousand years ago. Among other things, Tuan can use it to witness events as they happen many miles away. There are charms that can prevent the pendant from seeing you, but the magic will only protect you for a short time. We believe this pendant to be the weapon that aided Tuan in his defeat of the Brotherhood in the Great Battle of Dumnonia.'

'If Tuan knows what is happening as we do it, then how do we stand a chance of defeating him?' asked Falhinir worriedly. 'He will know exactly what our plans are.'

'The Pendant of Morrigan is limited in its power,' Hengest interjected, 'it can only be used for a limited period before its power is diminished and the vision fades.'

'We must be ready to leave soon,' said Sebastian, throwing the saddlebag over his shoulder, his knees buckling slightly under the weight, 'we have no way of knowing if Tuan knows you are here.'

'You are going to be joining me?' asked Falhinir taken aback.

'Someone will have to look after you!' Sebastian replied sharply.

On top of the cliffs high above the cave, the moonlight reflecting off their armour, the Dark Warriors were mounted upon their hellish steeds. 'There!' snorted one of the beasts, pointing to a dim light travelling towards the base of the cliffs. The beast's unholy companions nodded their heads in agreement, only the smoky breath of their horses lingered as they charged towards the beach.

Sebastian and Falhinir became aware of strong vibrations through the soles of their feet and ringing through the cliffs as horses' hooves clattered off the chalky surface. The Warrior's tore down towards them. Falhinir glanced upwards towards the cliff top and caught the moonlit reflection of the Warrior's armour. 'Dark Warriors!' he shouted to Sebastian.

'Quickly, we must move!' Sebastian yelled in reply.

There was no easy path to the beach from the cave, giving the pair no choice but to run down the steep slope that led to the shore.

'Move quicker boy!' urged Sebastian.

'I'm trying!' Falhinir angrily replied.

Sebastian tried to hurry Falhinir further but lost his footing. Toppling onto his back, he let out a startled shriek. Falhinir spun round on hearing Sebastian, only to find the old man sliding down the cliff towards him. He tried to outrun Sebastian, his arms and legs flailing wildly, but it was no good. Sebastian swept Falhinir's feet from beneath him, sending them both tumbling down the face of the cliffs like a pair of bowling balls towards the beach below, where they landed in a heap.

'Follow me!' shouted Sebastian. He led them to a small boat that was moored a short distance from the beach.

As they set off, Falhinir turned to the

shore, and through the moon's rays he could see the Dark Warriors in the distance. 'Quickly!' he shouted.

'I'm rowing as fast as I can' retorted the shaken little man.

'Well row bloody faster, they are gaining on us!' cried Falhinir, clearly frustrated at the old man's attempts at rowing.

Sebastian looked at Falhinir with a slight sneer. 'You're younger than I am! You row the bloody boat!' By now Sebastian was getting angry. He threw the oars down into the boat giving Falhinir no option but to take them up and row as hard as he could.

The dark warriors had realised that they were getting away and had flung themselves from their steeds and abandoned them to wait patiently on the shore below the cliffs. Since this was a popular fishing beach, there were all manner of fishing craft dragged up beyond the high waterline. It was a cinch for the Warriors to take the largest of the craft and shove it down to the expectant sea. The Warriors superior numbers and inhuman strength ensured their larger boat cut through the water far more swiftly than that of the inexperienced young boy and old man no matter how hard Falhinir rowed. Sebastian glanced toward the shore and was shocked to find the monsters gaining on them rapidly. It was only a matter of minutes before the Dark Warriors had caught up with them and had an iron clad fist firmly grasped to side of their small craft. Sebastian picked up the smaller of his two swords, not wanting to repeat the embarrassing incident in the cave, and began to randomly hack at the Warrior's armour.

'Get off!' Sebastian screamed at the beast, slashing wildly with his sword.

'Hit him!' ordered Falhinir.

'I am hitting him!' yelled Sebastian in angry response.

'Well hit him harder then!' Falhinir barked.

Sebastian, who was by now full of rage, gathered all his strength and raised his sword high above his head, almost skewering Falhinir with its sharp tip.

'Hey, be careful with that thing, you nearly bloody killed me!' he screamed.

'Just shut the hell up!' cried Sebastian as he thrust his blade through the eye slit of the Warrior's helmet, embedding the weapon deep in the beast's skull. The creature was dead before he hit the water.

Sebastian collapsed back into the boat exhausted. 'He's dead,' he reported to Falhinir, a little out of breath.

'Good!' Falhinir said sarcastically, nodding his head in Sebastian's direction, 'maybe you will be able to get rid of them a little more hastily!' In the melee the boats had drifted apart again and the relentless tide was pulling them further and further towards the shore. It was obvious that they were no match for the Warriors on land but the little boat they were on meant that the Warriors could only approach them one at a time. A small tactical advantage that they would be able to exploit until they could get to safety.

Sebastian quickly turned his head.

'Bugger me!' he exclaimed. 'Paddle harder boy!' he screamed looking back at Falhinir. 'They are gaining on us again! Get going! Oh, for crying...' Sebastian laid down on his front and began to use his arms as paddles.

'What the hell are you doing?' exclaimed Falhinir, thinking the old man had finally lost it completely.

Sebastian looked up at him scornfully. 'What does it look like I'm bloody doing? I'm getting us out of here!' he snapped in reply.

Having drifted a considerable distance toward the shore, both craft were at the mercy of the sand bars and hidden obstacles under the sea that so far both vessels had avoided. As the Warriors were much heavier in their craft, they were more vulnerable to such hazards that the small light boat the boys were on. After a short while they did not appear to be gaining on Sebastian and Falhinir and longer, as they started to pull away, it soon became obvious that they had become trapped on a sand bar caused by the unpredictable tide.

The fishing boat was stuck fast in the soft seabed and the more they struggled, the deeper into the sand they slipped. It did not take long for them to become so firmly wedged that they found that they could not move at all. Falhinir and Sebastian looked at each other for a brief moment. 'They're stuck in the sand!' they exclaimed in unison, relieved to be putting some distance between the stranded Warriors and their own much smaller and lighter little boat.

'Good thing they don't know where we are going,' said Sebastian with a sigh of relief.

'Yes, good thing,' agreed Falhinir, soon realising that *he* did not know where they were going either. 'Where exactly are we going to?' he asked after a moment's pause.

Sebastian got up off his stomach and sat upright. 'The ancient fort at Reculver, Hengest and Horsa told me that in order to get the next piece of the map we need to hold council with Vortigern. Strange.'

'The great King himself,' Falhinir muttered under his breath, for Vortigern was the first Saxon to be crowned King of all England over four hundred years before he was born. He had grown up hearing tales of the great Vortigern and his many adventures and battles. 'Why strange?'

'Do you not know your own people's history boy?' Sebastian asked indignantly. 'Hengest and Horsa had been brought to these lands by Vortigern as mercenaries from Jutland to aid him in his fight against the Picts. He thought that because of their noble father Whitgils, they would make great leaders for his armies. Which they did, but, when the fighting was done, Hengest encouraged others from his homeland to follow him here. Vortigern apparently did not take to this 'new invasion' and failed to make good his word on a payment that was due to Hengest and Horsa. Needless to say, the two seasoned mercenaries rebelled against him. It was during a confrontation with Vortigern at Aylesford that Horsa was killed.'

'How did Hengest die?' asked Falhinir.

'Having reigned over Kent for many

years, he eventually succumbed to old age.'

'I can see now how strange it is that there would be a form of alliance between the old enemies. Is it possible that they have forgiven one another in death?'

'Perhaps, we may well find out when we get to Reculver.'

'What of Hengest and Horsa now? Do they not accompany us?' Falhinir asked.

Sebastian looked back at the cliffs. 'They cannot leave the confines of the cliff. They can communicate with the Gods, but they can't pass the threshold of the cave.'

'Is that how they knew about the Pendant?'

Sebastian gave his young friend a serious look. 'There are many things in this world that harness incredible power, things that should never be allowed to be lost, for if they fall into dangerous hands, their actions could have terrible consequences for us all. When these items are used the energy, they create can be felt by many a warlock and shaman, even spirits. There are many entities who are aware the pendant has been activated today.'

Will we ever see them again?' Falhinir asked staring into the darkness of the channel.

'Who knows, boy? The memory of the great loss of life that resulted from the last encounter with Tuan filled him with dread. Sebastian was not convinced he would be so lucky this time, but then again, he was not much of an optimist. Born into a wealthy Canterbury family, his parents died when he was very young. Shortly afterwards he took up with the monks of St. Augustine's Abbey. It was here that he met Laravine, a monk who had not long converted to Christianity but still secretly held some of his Pagan beliefs. Laravine worked in the gardens and he had a more than working knowledge of nature and natural magic. It was the knowledge learnt from Laravine that brought Sebastian to the attention of several noblemen that belonged to a sacred Order. Sebastian begged the Brotherhood to accept him. When they finally did, he unwittingly entered a world of violence and suffering that would last for the next forty years. Whatever optimism, hope or ambition he had possessed was stolen from him with every wound he received and every life he took. It is for this reason, he was happy to live in the cave, isolated from the rest of humanity.

'How long will it take to get to Reculver, Sebastian?' asked Falhinir, noticing that Sebastian had drifted into a daydream.

'About a week with your useless rowing!' Sebastian replied jokingly. 'We should get some sleep and continue at dawn; it will not take long to reach the temple.'

Falhinir looked back towards the cliffs.

'Don't worry, we will be quite safe at this distance, for now,' assured Sebastian, placing his hand upon Falhinir's shoulder. He produced two animal skins from within his saddlebag and handed one to Falhinir.

Chapter III
In the Company of Kings

It was about midday by the time Falhinir and Sebastian had managed to manoeuvre their small boat along the coast to Reculver and drag it up onto the sandy beach. Sebastian looked up towards the fort, the crumbling relic of the once mighty Romans.

'What is this place?' asked Falhinir, looking up at the tall ruins that once stood proudly upon the cliffs of North Kent and out across the sea, a symbol of Roman dominance over the barbaric tribes of Britain. 'This was a fort built by the Romans,' replied Sebastian, clambering out of the boat. 'They used it for housing soldiers and as a beacon for ships that were headed for London and Rochester. Pick up the bags Falhinir, we must move quickly. Those Warriors can't be too far away.'

'Why was Vortigern buried in a Roman fort?' he asked. Sebastian shrugged his shoulders. ‘Don’t rightly know for sure. Nice views?’

Neither of them knew what to expect as they approached the ruined entrance of the fort. Nature had claimed this place for itself, the exposed interior was overgrown with ivy and a variety other fauna that was lightly dusted with sand from the nearby beach. Toward the far end of the open space was what would have been the altar only now it was partly in the open and exposed to the elements.

Other than the sound of the sea there was nothing but silence. There did not appear to be another soul around, with the exception of a few sea birds that had begun nesting along the tops of the walls. Falhinir felt a similar sensation of apprehension as when the Dark Warriors had appeared at Dover.

The wind’s chill began to bite as they approached the ancient altar stone. Falhinir held his hand to his face to shield his eyes from dust and sand as it was whipped into the air by the increasingly strong wind. Falhinir thought he was hearing things as faint whispers crept into his ears and Sebastian started as a voice from nowhere made him jump.

'You are of the Brotherhood, are you not?' said a man's voice in a low ethereal whisper. Falhinir spun round but still he could see no one. 'Who is there?' he asked nervously.

'I am the one you seek.' said the voice, this time much louder. 'My name is Vortigern. You wish to defeat the one whose name is evil. You must move swiftly; your whereabouts is known to him.'

Falhinir looked around as he spoke. 'I seek...'

'What you seek is the Book of Ceridwen,' interrupted Vortigern.

Suddenly the torches that hung either side of the ruined altar burst into flame and the voice beckoned Falhinir to approach. Cautiously he moved forward toward the lights, Sebastian taking hold of Falhinir's arm as he did so. Falhinir just

shook his head and removed Sebastian's hand. He walked up to the altar, where the voice commanded him to take one of the lights. As he pulled one of the torches from the wall, the ground beneath him gave way and Falhinir plunged into the darkness below. Sebastian dashed over to the hole in the ground grabbing the other torch as he passed. He swung the torch above the void and peered in. He could see Falhinir picking himself up from amongst the rubble of what had previously been the floor.
'Falhinir, are you alright?' he shouted.

'I'm not hurt!' Falhinir cried in reply, choking a little on the dust that filled the air.

As the air settled, he picked up the torch. He found himself in an ancient burial chamber that had been built into the chalky cliff, and he could see that the walls were lined with stone sarcophagi. Looking around, Falhinir noticed the names of some of the first Kings of Kent etched into the sides of the caskets, Hengest and Horsa amongst them.

'What's down there?' asked Sebastian.

'A huge tomb!' Falhinir shouted in reply.

'Hold on! I'm coming down!' cried Sebastian, as he slowly clambered through the hole in the ground before him. Hanging for a few moments, he dropped down into the vault.

They explored the tomb in awe. 'I had no idea this was here,' said Sebastian, his fingers tracing Horsa's inscription.

'Over here!' Falhinir shouted to Sebastian.

Trotting toward Falhinir, Sebastian could see that there was a coffin standing alone in the centre of the vault. Over four feet in height, it was intricately carved with scenes of many battles, and four hideous gargoyles with tortured faces protruded from each of the four corners.

'Who does this belong to?' Sebastian asked.

Blowing the dust from the capstone, Falhinir raised his torch. The dim flame revealed the inscription:

ᚹᛟᚱᛏᛁᚷᛖᚱᚾ

ᚲᛁᛜ ᛟᚠ ᚨᛚᛚ ᛒᚱᛁᛏᛟ ᚾᛊ

VORTIGERN

KING OF ALL BRITONS

Falhinir and Sebastian looked at each other. 'What now?' Sebastian asked.

'We open it,' Falhinir replied, beginning to shove the heavy lid. Together they managed to push the capstone to one side, revealing the remains of the King. They couldn't help but take a few moments to view the body in all its splendour. The corpse was adorned with fantastic jewels. A lavish helmet, complete with an elaborate face covering, a gift to the dead king, rested on top of his skull. A long sword had been placed in his hands, the blade leading towards the feet, and a circular wooden shield lay over the blade, decorated with studs of pure gold. Falhinir spied a parchment resting among the skeleton's ribs, protruding through the body's decaying garments. Clearing away the dust and cobwebs, he carefully retrieved it. As he unravelled it, he realised he was looking at the second part of the map.

Vortigern's voice rang out once more. 'Follow this map to the Forest Lands of Middle Anglia. There you will find the bearer of the final piece.'

'Who is it we seek?' asked Sebastian nervously.

'When you are near, he will seek you out. Now, go!' said Vortigern, his voice shaking the very foundations of the building.

'Watch out!' cried Falhinir as pieces of rubble came crashing down, sealing the hole in the roof of the vault. Sebastian cast around to see if there was another way out, but the void had been completely filled with debris from above.

'What do we do now!' he shrieked, looking at Falhinir.

'Look!' Falhinir yelled, as a long line of torches ignited in front of them. 'This way,' he said.

The lights pointed the way to a small passageway carved from the rock. Looking at each other they cautiously entered the long corridor.

'What do you suppose this is Sebastian?' Falhinir asked.

'I think it is the pathway used to bring the bodies to their final resting place,' the old man replied.

As they continued forward, they could see a small chink of light in far in front of them. As they got closer, they could see it was a small crack in the cliff face. Breaking through, they discovered that they were just yards from the beach and could see their boat resting on the sand a short distance away.

Once they had reached the

sanctuary of their little boat, Falhinir surveyed the map; he followed the trail with his finger as he described it to Sebastian. 'According to this, the nearest place to pick up supplies is London,' he said, 'we may also be able to lose our "friends" a bit more easily in the city.'

'And how do you suppose we pay for these supplies, moneybags?' asked Sebastian.

'I'm sure a solution will present itself when we get there, anyway, if I may continue?'

Sebastian nodded his head. 'From London we make our way North to the great forests of the Middle Lands, and that is as far as the map goes.'

'Great!' exclaimed Sebastian sarcastically. 'So, it's nice and easy then, not only do we have Dark Warriors after us, we have to try and gain money in a strange city and then brave bandits and wolves in the forests where no sod lives! And what do we do when we get there, do you think?' Sebastian gave Falhinir a look of uncertainty. He had no answers for the little man. They had come this far and had been lucky, how much longer was their luck likely to continue, he wondered. He was not about to give up now, even if the next part of the journey would take them far away from his beloved Kent. 'Come on, we'd better be on our way before we start to lose daylight.' he sighed.

Falhinir took one last look at the great towers on the cliffs only to find that they too were now ruined, the source of the rubble filling the hole in the crypt now becoming clear. They rowed in shifts between them and steadily made progress towards the estuary, eventually joining the few trading vessels, heading toward the great city of London.

The pair could not believe how busy the ports along the riverbanks were as they made their way upriver towards what seemed to be the centre of the city. There were ships with goods from all over the world. Merchants were selling just about anything; skins from Africa, bead necklaces from the Mediterranean, and delicacies from Gaul.

'We should be able to make some more money and pick up supplies easily here,' Falhinir muttered to Sebastian.

'Perhaps,' Sebastian replied cautiously.

Falhinir glanced toward the shore, where on the far side of the bank he could make out an inn with room for them to moor the boat. 'We have enough to pay for shelter for the night,' he said, counting the coins in his purse, and we can look for work and supplies tomorrow.'

'The only thing I'm looking for right now is a jug of mead!' said Sebastian enthusiastically.

Once they had moored the boat, they made their way inside the inn. As soon as they opened the door the whole room fell silent and every eye immediately targeted the pair. The door began to creak loudly as they closed it behind them. If they were not feeling conspicuous enough, the floorboards appeared to scream in pain with every step they took. With more bravado than they felt, they approached the landlord, who was greedily guzzling a jug of ale. 'We would like a room for the night,' asked Falhinir, trying not to sound too unnerved, every stare feeling like a knife piercing his back.

'Follow me,' said the intimidating landlord with a deep growling voice. And with that, conversations around the tap room resumed. They felt like they had passed some sort of test as they made their way up the stairs behind the large backside of the innkeeper to a small room above the bar that overlooked the oily black waters of the river and their little boat moored alongside the quay.

The pair found it no hard task to fall asleep that night. It was the first real bed Falhinir had slept in for over a month. They rested in the relative comfort, content that the Warriors would not be able to find them so easily in the bustle of the city.

Chapter IV

London

The cry of a lone cockerel finally awoke Falhinir from deep slumber. He turned over and looked across the room towards Sebastian, who was snoring heavily, happily dreaming about the food he had seen being landed from the cargo ships the previous evening. However, Sebastien's happy slumbers were rudely interrupted as he awoke to a glancing blow on his head. He leapt from of his bed, looking this way and that, trying to find the source of the blow and shake the sleep from his fuddled brain. 'Dark Warriors are here!' he cried, reaching for his sword.

He looked across to Falhinir, only to discover that he was gently shaking and loud chuckling was emanating from beneath his blanket. He then noticed a familiar leather shoe lying on the floor beside his bed. 'You want to grow up a bit my boy!' he shouted angrily. 'You'll be the death of me!' Falhinir emerged from within his blanket and rolled over laughing. Sebastian was clearly not as amused. He walked over to the window, muttering to himself; 'I don't know, here, in a strange and dangerous place with a gang of unearthly beings after us and all this young fool can do is sod about!' Of course, thought Sebastien, that was why he could sod about; because he *was* young and had no concept of the dangers that lay ahead.

'Come on Sebastian,' said Falhinir, noticing that Sebastian was angry with him; 'you must admit that we are pretty safe here, and it is about time we had something to laugh about.'

Sebastian turned to Falhinir. 'Up you get, we have to find a way of making money and getting us some supplies so that we can get the hell out of here. The sooner we get to Ceridwen the better.'

Sometime later, after a bowl of watery porridge and a thin mug of ale, begrudgingly supplied by the somewhat bleary-eyed innkeeper, they stepped out of the inn. The land side of the inn opened onto a busy narrow street. Sebastien and Falhinir, narrowly avoiding being hit by a heavily laden horse and cart as it hurried on its way to the riverside causing anyone in their way to dive for safety from the clattering hooves and large cartwheels in such a tight street. 'I've never seen so many people in any one place before,' Falhinir whispered into Sebastian's ear. The port at Romney was never this frantic. There were so many ships. Vessels of all sizes and shapes were lined up along the riverbank jostling for space.

'Stay close to me lad and you'll be alright,' said Sebastian with more reassurance than he felt.

They had been walking the streets for almost an hour, asking anybody that looked like they had money if they wanted to hire any help, but to no avail. Then, as they turned into yet another narrow street, the raucous cheering and shouting of a large crowd filled the air. They looked at each other and after a brief discussion both agreed that where a large number of people were to be found was a better chance of finding work. They headed in the general direction of the cheering until it led them to yet another narrow, cobbled street. Peering down the road, they could see a large gathering of people. The pair just glanced at each other, nodded, and made their way towards the huge crowd.

When they got to the centre of the commotion, they realised that there was some form of contest taking place. Sebastian growled unhappily, he was far from impressed both with the contest or the contestants.

'What is it?' Falhinir asked.

'It's a contest to see who is the strongest in battle. There are different fields of combat. Some fight with swords, others use their fists or wrestle like animals.'

Falhinir placed his hand on his sword that hung from his waist, hidden by his tunic. 'Don't even think about it boy!' Sebastian snapped sharply, firmly grabbing Falhinir's hand. 'This was a crazy idea thought of by the bloody Romans. Only fools participate in such lunacy, take my advice and stay well away from games such as these.'

Falhinir looked on silently. There were events of all kinds, archery, sword-fighting and fist-fighting too, plus some he had never seen before. Falhinir knew that he had the skills needed to win some of the contests, most notably the archery and possibly with the sword-fights. He had been praised for his skill with the iron swords the blacksmith in Romney had made for the adolescent lads in the village to practice with. He knew that the sword at his belt would make his skill even more impressive as the blade was light, balanced and had felt like an extension of his arm. He was fascinated by the impressive swordplay being demonstrated before him and as one man arose triumphant from the fight, the crowd cheered as loudly as they could. Falhinir was stunned by the huge purse of coins awarded to the victor for his efforts. He leaned into Sebastian's ear. 'I'll be back shortly,' he said.

Sebastian turned to ask his companion where he was going, but Falhinir had gone. Sebastian just caught a glimpse of him disappearing into the crowd. 'That boy has too many crazy ideas.' Sebastian muttered to himself. As there was nothing else he could do but wait for his young friend to return, he found himself a seat high upon a wall overlooking the arena. He might as well watch the action whilst he waited.

Meanwhile, Falhinir had left the old man to search for a means of entering the contest. As Falhinir wandered through the crowds, he suddenly felt a firm and persuasive grip on his shoulder from behind. His first thought was Dark Warrior's but this was something else.

'What are you looking for here boy?' said the stranger, in a sullen voice that sent a shiver of fear through Falhinir.

'What concern is it of yours?' Falhinir replied, looking down at the stranger's hand.

'That sword you carry, how did you come

by it?'

Falhinir glanced down to see that his sword's scabbard was protruding from beneath his tunic, displaying the Cross of the Order. 'It belonged to my uncle. What does it matter to you?'

Falhinir turned on his heel to find himself in the shadow of a tall, well-built man with chin-length hair and a scar upon his cheek. He had the face of a man with much experience about him, hard and rugged. Pulling back his cloak, he revealed that he too had an identical sword hanging from his waist. 'My father was a knight of the Brotherhood of the Sword.'

'As was my Uncle,' replied Falhinir assertively.

'My father was killed at the Battle of Dumnonia. I assume that is where your uncle died as well. But you don't look old enough to remember that.'

'Battle of Dumnonia?' Falhinir answered with a puzzled look, 'no, my uncle died in the marshes of Kent a few months ago.'

'Then I can see we have much to talk

about" the stranger replied, 'I am competing shortly, meet me in the tavern around the corner after the tournament, we can talk then'

'Wait, do you know how I too can enter the contest?' asked Falhinir.

The stranger turned to Falhinir. 'Don't be foolish, it is dangerous here.' Before Falhinir could answer him, he disappeared into the crowd.

Undeterred, Falhinir pushed his way through to the front of the spectators. He could see the stranger and another competitor were about to engage in combat. Falhinir looked on, impressed, as his new acquaintance was drawn into a fierce contest. He was amazed at how quickly the mysterious fellow could move, and it was obvious that he was no stranger to this sport. The crowd cheered and howled with every blow that he struck. During the course of the afternoon, there was not one single competitor that could beat him.

The crowd cheered frantically as the

stranger's last opponent fell upon the dusty ground and a large man rushed out to congratulate him. 'Are there no more challengers?' he cried. He was met by silence. Then as if propelled by an external force Falhinir stepped to the edge of the arena. 'I will challenge him!' he exclaimed. After a moment of complete silence, the entire arena burst into gales of laughter. Angrily Falhinir stormed into the arena, 'I am going to fight this man!' and the crowd settled from their laughter, impressed with the courage of the youngster but anticipating a bloodbath nevertheless. The fight was begun.

Sebastian, who had been observing the tournament from his vantage point, had enjoyed seeing the stranger beating all comers before beginning to notice something different about his style. The stance and tactics of the stranger were familiar to him and the grip and shape of his weapon was noticeably superior to those of his opponents. It wasn't long before

Sebastian realised he knew exactly what type of sword it was and where the stranger had learned to fight like that. Suddenly he could see Falhinir entering the arena and began shouting and waving his arms frantically. 'Stop, you must not fight! Don't be a bloody...' Just as Sebastian jumped to his feet, he missed his footing on the wall, slipped and fell to the hard ground with an almighty thud. He saw no further part of what happened afterwards, having rendered himself completely unconscious from the fall.

'Alright, boy,' said Falhinir's opponent, 'let's see what you've got. Bring the boy some armour!' he shouted. Two men rushed over to Falhinir and equipped him with a woollen gambeson and a mail tunic. He found it difficult to move in the heavy padding and mail, as his opponent charged headlong at him. Falhinir spun to avoid the blade of his attacker's sword, but could not move fast enough with the added weight of the armour. He almost fell to the ground as he received a tremendous blow to the top of his right arm, which sent shockwaves surging through his body. He gathered all his strength and made to move in for an attack. His opponent stood firm, anticipating the oncoming assault, adjusting his stance to absorb the impact. Falhinir raised his sword high into the air and brought it down as hard as he could. The stranger too, lifted his weapon above his head to block the expected trajectory of the blade. Seeing that the stranger had acted predictably to parry his blow Falhinir altered the thrust of his sword, sending the flat of the blade crashing into the stranger's side.

The onlookers cheered as each of the protagonists had received a blow from one another. By now Falhinir was becoming a little more accustomed to the extra weight of the cumbersome armour and was finding he could move about more freely in it. Then, just as he thought he may be gaining a slight advantage over his older opponent, the stranger came at him with a massive overhead swing. Falhinir lifted his sword above his head to absorb the blow and for the first time in the contest the two blades met metal to metal. There was a blinding flash of light as the two pieces of steel touched and a clear ringing sound as sonorous as any bell echoed around the arena. The pair were locked together for a few seconds as sparks began to emerge from each of the touching blades. Suddenly they were both flung to opposite ends of the arena by a tremendous force that caused both combatants to hit to the ground, momentarily stunned. The two identical swords clattered into the dirt of the arena, their blades smouldering.

The crowd fell silent; bewildered and amazed by the spectacle they had just witnessed. The only sound Falhinir could hear as he came too was that of Sebastian yelling. The small man had woken with a ringing in his ears. Thinking it was from his fall, it had taken a moment to realise that it was coming from the arena itself. He could see Falhinir lying dazed at the nearside of the dusty ring. Running over, still nursing the bump on his head, he knelt beside his friend and helped him to sit upright. 'What the hell happened?' asked a confused Falhinir. Sebastian would not answer him, and after making sure his young friend was none the worse for his encounter, he got up and walked towards the still smoking weapons. He stood gazing for a few seconds at the benign steel that had just demonstrated such enormous power. He was joined by Falhinir and his opponent, who just looked at each other bewilderingly.

'The swords,' said Sebastian, 'the swords of the Brotherhood cannot be used in anger against one another. They were made to be a force for good, it is forbidden for them to fight against their own kind. If you had continued for any longer, there is a very good chance you would have both been killed.'

'We have to talk,' said the stranger to Sebastian, 'there is an inn not far from here where we can speak.'

The arena was still stunned into an

uneasy silence. People had already begun to disperse. No further combat would take place this afternoon. Falhinir picked up both the weapons and discarded the borrowed armour. The stranger collected his winnings and the small party left together.

It was almost nightfall when they entered the inn, for the sun did not linger in the sky for long at this time of year. The two friends were glad to replace the autumn chill with the heat of a roaring fire. As they took their places around a large well-scrubbed table, they were joined by the stranger and his younger companion. He was a man of more than six feet in height and probably wasn't much older than Falhinir. He wore the garments of a soldier which were shrouded by a heavy cloak of black cloth. His thick, dark hair touched his shoulders, and he too had the look of a man who had had to become accustomed to spending long periods of time exposed to the elements. Beneath his short beard were the defined features of a man that had seen more than a little of life's darker side.

As Falhinir and the younger man-made eye contact, he found a look of familiarity staring back at him, almost as if he were looking at his future self, and then the older man spoke; 'My name is Arnor of Merion, and this is Æthelwulf of Warwick. We are knights of the court of King Æthelred of Mercia.'

'I am Falhinir of Romney and this is Sebastian. What brings you to London?'

'Our Kingdom is locked in war,' said Arnor soberly, 'and Æthelred has sent us upon a diplomatic mission to gain allies that would help our cause. We have recently held council with Ecgbryht of Kent. We now begin our return journey home to Mercia.'

'I am interested to know how you came by that sword,' asked Sebastian, looking at Arnor with a suspicious squint.

'It belonged to my father.' replied the older knight.

'Who was he?' enquired Falhinir.

'Uther of Merion,' Arnor replied.

'Uther,' Sebastian pondered, 'I

remember him,' he continued a short while later. 'He was one of the first to join the Order and, if I remember correctly, he was of Celtic origin and a great swordsman. I can see some of your father's skill in you.'

Arnor's eyes opened wide as he looked at Sebastian, eyeing the little man uneasily. Uther had been killed when Arnor was Falhinir's age and he had been searching most of his life for someone who could shed some light on what kind of man his father was. He was desperate to learn more about him, to know some insight into his own origins, but how could this strange little man have known him. 'How do you know of my father, old man?'

'I knew your father because I taught him to fight. I trained all the knights of the Brotherhood.' replied Sebastian.

'Were you there, when he died?' asked Arnor, looking Sebastian squarely in the eye. He was unsure how such as small man could have trained the knights of the Brotherhood but his instincts told him Sebastian was speaking the truth.

'Yes,' replied Sebastian, 'I was there. Many brave men died that day.'

Falhinir stared at the two men with a look of confusion. 'What are you talking about?' he asked.

'The Battle of Dumnonia,' replied Arnor.

'You mentioned that before,' said Falhinir, 'what was that?'

Arnor looked to Falhinir. 'It was the day the Brotherhood of the Sword faced Tuan and his forces.'

Arnor looked back at Sebastian. 'I do not know the exact details of the battle, perhaps you could enlighten us?'

Sebastian ordered four jugs of ale, made himself comfortable beside the fireplace, and looked around the inn. When he was convinced their conversation would not be overheard, he proceeded to tell the story of the battle.

'Almost twenty years ago the Knights of the Brotherhood, along with their allies, faced Tuan in Dumnonia. It was a vicious conflict and most of those present on the battlefield field died that day. We managed to destroy much of Tuan's army, but we were not strong enough to defeat the sorcerer himself. Not even Ceridwen could stop Tuan, and even though she managed to drain him of much of his powers, he murdered fourteen of the Knights of the Order that had led the army against him. Of the few people that survived that day only Falhinir's uncle, Ceridwen and I were left from the Brotherhood, the rest had been slaughtered or died shortly afterwards of their wounds. Unfortunately, Ceridwen was so weakened by the fighting that she was unable to kill Tuan and he retreated further to the west. Although his powers were seriously diminished, he has been gaining in strength ever since and he will soon be restored to his full powers again.'

'Why does he so want to destroy us?' asked Falhinir.

'Revenge,' replied Sebastian soberly, 'he wants revenge for the invasion of his homeland which has happened many times over several centuries. Five hundred years ago he launched his first attack upon this land, but he was beaten back by Ceridwen and the other Ancients, along with the Roman armies of the Emperor Hadrian. It was then that he was first imprisoned by Cerdiwen, but somehow, twenty years ago, he managed to escape his enchantments and launch another attack, that culminated in the Battle of Dumnonia. Everyone had believed that Tuan had been defeated, until his Dark Warrior's caught up with your uncle.'

'What happened to your uncle?' Arnor asked Falhinir.

Falhinir began to recount his tale; 'Four months ago my uncle returned to our settlement. He had been away for many years, but no sooner had he got to the village, when twelve of Tuan's Dark Warriors set upon our homes. Somehow, they knew that my uncle was there and began to destroy the entire settlement. They would have killed everyone if it were not for my uncle. He fought bravely, killing one of them, but there were too many and they tortured and murdered him. I am his nephew and *that* is why they are after us. They believed him to be the last in the bloodline of the Knights of the Order and did not know about me until I took hold of the sword, although it is strange that they do not know about you.'

'They must think you are already dead or never existed,' interjected Sebastian.

Arnor knew only too well that Falhinir had spoken the truth. The Warriors had come to his own village, shortly after the great battle and destroyed everyone and everything that they could find. It was by pure chance that Arnor had been visiting a friend in a neighbouring village the day they had come. 'And what are you doing in London?' he asked, taking a large sip of his ale.

'We are here to gather supplies for our journey north to the Forest Lands, and to seek solace amongst the busy streets,' explained Falhinir, 'the Dark Warriors that are chasing us know that we are seeking the book. We wish to use it to destroy their master and they are intent on stopping us getting anywhere near it"

'Book?' enquired Æthelwulf, who up until now had shown little interest in the conversation.

'You have heard of the great witch Ceridwen?' Falhinir asked Æthelwulf, slightly puzzled as to why this man had remained silent until now.

'Yes. She is a powerful witch, an Ancient, but I thought that the book was just a myth.'

Falhinir pierced Æthelwulf with a clear gaze. 'No myth, the book is real, and so is she. The book is the only thing that will enable us to finally defeat Tuan before he regains his strength. God only knows what will happen if we fail.'

Æthelwulf leant forward onto the table. 'How do you expect to find the book when no one knows where Ceridwen is to be found?'

'We have our means,' Sebastian interjected.

Æthelwulf sat back in his chair and

sipped his ale.

Falhinir looked at Arnor. 'Would you care to join us for part of the journey, at least until such time as we are close to the lands of Mercia? We would certainly welcome your assistance.' The boy was certainly impetuous, thought Sebastian.

Sebastian stood up, grabbed Falhinir by his shoulders, and pulled him into a corner. 'Excuse us for a moment,' Sebastian said loudly, followed by a forced smile. 'What the hell are you doing?' he whispered angrily, turning back to Falhinir, 'we do not know these people, if the book was to fall into the wrong hands it would be just as catastrophic as letting Tuan run free!'

Falhinir roughly removed Sebastian's hands from his tunic. 'I think we can trust Arnor. He will want to avenge the death of his father, and they both know these lands far better than we do. They have travelled far to get here and have probably travelled a great deal more than that in the service of their King.'

Sebastian stared Falhinir in the eye. 'You

may be right, but what about that other fellow? We know nothing about him!'

Falhinir glanced over at the pair, 'Yes, he is a quiet one but I feel we ought to trust them both. Besides, Ceridwen will have possession of the book. She is the only one who knows how to use it properly, after all she did write the thing! She is a powerful witch; she won't just hand it over to anyone who asks'

Sebastian pulled Falhinir close, pointing a finger at him. 'Alright, we'll ask them if they want to join us, but if anything should happen it will be your responsibility to resolve any wrongdoing!' Falhinir nodded silently in agreement, hoping that his instincts would not fail him.

'Sorry about that,' said Falhinir, feeling rather embarrassed as he and Sebastian resumed their places at the table. 'We would like to know your answer, will you join us?'

'We have decided to join you on your quest,' Arnor said solemnly.

'Thank you,' Falhinir replied excitedly,

'and once we reach Mercia, we will part company.'

'You misunderstand,' Æthelwulf interjected, 'we have decided to assist you in your quest to find the book and defeat Tuan.'

'Why would you do such a thing?' asked Falhinir.

'There is much at stake,' Arnor replied soberly, 'both Æthelwulf and myself have seen much war and death. By helping you we may create an opportunity for the kingdoms of these islands to unite together and maybe save many lives in the future. We also have certain limited resources at our disposal, that may prove useful.'

Falhinir and Sebastian finished their ale and stood up. 'We must leave early tomorrow, but we have not yet found ourselves a form of transport or gathered our supplies,' said Falhinir, picking up is tunic 'We still have much to do.'

'I will take care of that,' replied the younger of the two knights.

'Thank you, Æthelwulf' said Falhinir,

'then it is settled. We will meet again in the square by the North gate at dawn.'

Just as they began to walk away Arnor threw a purse of money on the table.

'What's this?' asked Sebastian, eyeing the small leather pouch eagerly.

'This is your half of the winnings, Falhinir. I think it was a draw, don't you?'

Falhinir smiled, picked up the purse and Arnor and Æthelwulf looked at each other with a slight grin as Falhinir and Sebastian left the inn. The pair of knights may have looked like they would rather run you through than look at you, but they did have kind hearts. They instantly took a liking to Falhinir and knew he would need as much help as they could give him, if not more, if he was to defeat Tuan.

As Falhinir and Sebastian walked the cold streets, they began to get an uneasy feeling, and for good reason. Cloaked in the darkness of a narrow alley there stood two Warriors. They had been waiting for Falhinir and Sebastian to appear for some time, having discovered their small vessel earlier that evening. The beasts had waited for the companions to return to the inn and waited for them to go inside. The fire had almost died completely as the innkeeper chivvied the last of his ale soaked regulars to leave. At last the taproom was silent, it had been a busy day and leather drinking jugs and stone flagons were strewn about the tables. The only sound that could be heard was that of the wind whistling as it blew down the chimney, gently stirring the flames of the last few logs that lay within the blackened hearth. The innkeeper, not adverse to sampling his own wares, was in need of a rest, as he so often was at this time of night. Clearing up the bar was a chore he detested. Perhaps another jug of ale and a little sit down before he tackled the last of the bar jobs would make it more bearable, he reasoned. So, he drew himself a jug of ale and lowered his ample behind into a comfy bench down beside the fireplace. Suddenly he was startled by a loud crash, causing him to throw his jug into the air, spilling beer everywhere. What a waste, he thought as the liquid seeped between the flagstones. Turning to the source of the racket, he could see that his front door had been ripped clean off its hinges. There, in the doorway, stood a menacing figure in pockmarked rusty black armour.

Falhinir and Sebastian, who had only been in bed a short while, were awoken by a commotion coming from downstairs. They crept down the landing and stood silently at the top of the stairs. As they listened intently, they could only make out the flickering shadows cast by the fire on the opposite wall.

'What do you want?' the innkeeper hollered indignantly, still thinking of the wasted ale.

The figure did not speak, but approached him silently.

'Get out of here!' the fat barman shouted as he drew a dagger. 'Come any closer and I'll stick you!'

The dying flames let out one last burst of

light that illuminated the fearsome eyes of a Dark Warrior, and the innkeeper's soul was instantly filled with terror. He changed his tune immediately 'What do you want?' he repeated, his voice trembling.

'Nothing from you!' the beast replied, drawing its sword and advancing on the trembling landlord.

From the landing above, Falhinir saw the shadow of a decapitated corpse crumple onto the flagstones. 'Bloody hell!' he exclaimed, trying not to raise his voice.

'What is it boy?' Sebastian whispered; his view of the room below obscured by Falhinir.

'I think they've caught up with us!' Falhinir whispered urgently.

A look of shock came over Sebastian's face. 'Well then let's get the hell out of here!'

'Too bloody right!' agreed Falhinir, leaping to his feet, 'we'll have to find another way out though and fast!'

They could hear the beast's footsteps coming up the stairs behind them as they retreated into their room and grabbed their belongings. Falhinir tried to shut the door, hoping to buy the a few more seconds but it was too late, the Warrior was in the next room. 'The window!' he whispered loudly to Sebastian. Falhinir went to the window and squinted out. Their little boat was moored on the quayside where they had left it the day before. He turned and faced his friend. 'Sebastian! Will you *please* get a ruddy move on! The only way out is through this window, our boat is just down there.'

'I don't want to jump into the cold, dirty river!' exclaimed Sebastian with a slight shriek.

Falhinir grabbed his arm. 'Would you rather stay here with that Warrior?'

Sebastian could not argue with his young friend. 'Alright, I'm convinced!'

Falhinir leaped into the dark, icy cold water. Looking back at the inn, illuminated by the broken moonlight, Falhinir could see Sebastian placing one leg out of the window. 'Quickly, jump!' Falhinir shouted as he scrambled to pull himself into their boat. He flopped in wetly and looked around to help his friend. There had been no second splash so he cast around to find the little old man. When he looked back up at the window, he could see that the Warrior had gotten hold of Sebastian and was trying to drag him back into the room. Falhinir immediately took hold of his bow and two arrows that were still in the bottom of the boat. Remarkable really, he thought, I would have expected someone to have pinched them. I really should take greater care to gather up my things and keep them about me, he mused, now was not the time to panic or aim wildly. He took aim at the illuminated window with measured detachment.

'Come back in boy, or I'll kill your friend!' the Dark Warrior threatened in its unnatural voice, holding a blade to Sebastian's throat. Falhinir trained his arrow at the Warrior.

'Not bloody likely!' he shouted, letting go of the first arrow. It whizzed past

Sebastian's head, nicking his ear, and piercing the neck of the creature, swiftly followed by the second arrow. Sebastian looked down at Falhinir in terror. 'Stop firing arrows at me!' he cried. The Warrior stumbled back in confusion, reaching for the arrows firmly embedded in its throat. He let his grip loosen on the old man allowing him to wrestle free. The creature didn't realise that he was mortally wounded and continued to paw at the arrows in its throat as it staggered back into the room. Sebastian was at the window.

'Jump!' yelled Falhinir.

As Sebastian leapt from the window, with the last of its dying strength, the Warrior lunged at the window, grabbing Sebastian's falling ankle. The pair plunged into the murky water. Falhinir manhandled Sebastian into the boat as swiftly as he could. The Warrior, had lost hold of the escaping Sebastien as they fell and landed some way away from the boat with a second splash. The heavy armour pulled the creature down toward the riverbed, the arrows slipping finally beneath the rippling water of the now silent river. Falhinir smiled at his friend. 'You didn't know I was that good with a bow, did you?'

Sebastian looked at him sternly. 'You nearly bloody killed me, and look at what you did!' he shouted, wiping a little blood from his ear.

Falhinir picked up one of the oars, ignoring Sebastian, who was holding out his hand, trying to draw attention to a tiny speck of blood upon his extended forefinger. 'Stop bloody moaning, will you? And pick up that other oar! We don't know how many more of those things are in the city.' He looked up into the sky. 'The sun will be up in a couple of hours; it will then be time to meet Arnor and Æthelwulf. It will probably be safer if we stay in the boat and out in the middle of the river until dawn.'

Sebastian was awoken by watery sunlight beaming through the dull clouds that littered the sky. 'Wake up Falhinir, it is time.' They rowed the boat to the edge of the riverbank, pulled their hoods over their faces, disembarked and made their way to the North gate. 'I'll be glad to see the back of that bloody boat.' Sebastian said with a rueful grin. Twice, now the little vessel had saved them from the Warriors.

A short walk through the early morning bustle of the twisting London streets brought them to the rendezvous point. Sebastian and Falhinir could see Arnor and Æthelwulf in the distance. The two knights nodded their heads in recognition.

'We must move quickly,' said Falhinir anxiously as he approached the pair, 'we are not safe here. I will explain on the way, is the transport ready?'

Æthelwulf glanced at Arnor. 'I'll take care of it now,' he said, disappearing into the early morning throng.

'I must assume you two had an eventful evening,' asked Arnor, 'and what happened to your ear Sebastian?'

'That boy!' he pointed angrily. 'You have

no idea what he is capable of!'

Æthelwulf returned with two horses. 'How are two horses going to accommodate the four of us?' enquired Sebastian.

'Our steeds are with the farrier,' Æthelwulf replied.

'They have been packed with supplies and are waiting for us on the edge of town,' added Arnor, 'we should head there now.'

Once they were outside the farrier's and while Arnor and Æthelwulf were collecting their horses, Falhinir and Sebastian consulted the map. They trusted their new friends, but not quite enough to reveal that they were in possession of a map that would lead directly to Ceridwen's whereabouts. 'According to this, we must travel deep into the forests of Middle Anglia.' Falhinir told his friend, following the trail with his finger.

'Then where do we go from there?' asked Sebastian.

'That's it,' said Falhinir, realising the trail ended in the forest. He tucked the map back into his tunic, 'I assume we collect the next part of the map there, and the map just leads us in the direction of the forest. Do you remember what Vortigern said? Whoever we have to meet will find *us*.'

Sebastian mounted his horse. 'I guess we go to the forest then.' he said, sounding rather fed up about the vague instructions they were expected to follow.

Arnor and Æthelwulf joined them already mounted on stout capable looking steeds, laden with saddlebags. 'We must travel to the forests of Middle Anglia,' said Falhinir as he jumped upon his own, less encumbered but equally fresh-looking horse.

Æthelwulf looked at Falhinir forebodingly. 'We know the forests of Middle Anglia; they are dangerous, full of thieves and murderers.'

'What possible reason could we have for going there?' Arnor asked, not entirely convinced it was a good idea.

'There is someone who we must meet there.' replied Falhinir.

'Who?' asked Æthelwulf.

'I don't know yet.' Falhinir answered.

Before Æthelwulf could question Falhinir further, the sound of hooves galloping against the cobbled streets could be heard in the distance. Sebastian looked at Falhinir. 'I think they may be following us again,' he said.

Falhinir nodded in agreement. 'We must go!'

'Those friends you mentioned?' asked Æthelwulf.

'How did you guess?' shouted Falhinir as he dug into the horse's flanks with his feet and urged the beast to hurry. They galloped out of the city as fast as they dared without drawing unnecessary attention to themselves and raced towards the open countryside, putting as much distance between themselves and the pursuing Warriors as they could.

'They're coming!' yelled Sebastian. 'And we are more than a little outnumbered!' he continued.

'There is some thick woodland in the distance!' cried Æthelwulf. 'We will be able to hide in there.' He looked over his shoulder. 'What the hell are they? I've never seen anything like them before!' He did not get a reply.

Riding as hard as they could, they followed a path that led them into the woodland. 'Down here, quickly!' yelled Æthelwulf.

They charged into the thick of the wood, where they found a couple of fallen trees. They dismounted and the horses were laid in some undergrowth, Sebastian stayed with them to ensure that they made no sound, Falhinir and the others peered from behind the huge oak tree trunks. The tall trees that blocked most of the daylight rustled as the wind blew between them and in the dull light Falhinir could just make out the outlines of the Warriors.

They walked their horses through the dense vegetation of the forest floor, swiping at the undergrowth with their swords. The beasts snorted and snarled but their hiding place was secure and they were not found. The frustrated Warriors turned to leave the forest furious they had lost the trail of the knights and would not be able to search the bleak woodland in its entirety.

The four companions breathed a sigh of relief as they heard the horses riding off into the distance.

'So, they were the Dark Warriors you mentioned,' said Æthelwulf, mounting his horse.

Falhinir looked at him and nodded. 'Yes, and I don't think that will be the last we see of them either. They were the creatures that destroyed my settlement and killed my uncle.'

'How did they know you were in London?' asked Arnor.

Sebastian looked over at him. 'If we knew that, perhaps we could lose them more easily,' he said.

'Not far from here is a ferry crossing, we will need to get across the river soon, if we are to have a full days' riding,' Æthelwulf informed the others. With that, they all mounted up and rode off warily in the direction of the crossing, every so often glancing behind them hoping they were not being followed.

Once safely aboard the ferry, Falhinir stood pondering their situation. Arnor's question was bothering him. *Just how did the Dark Warriors know where to find them?* He knew there wasn't something quite right about this. We had lost the Warriors below the cliffs in Dover. How had they found them again in London so easily? There were hundreds of little boats like theirs. How had the Warriors struck so lucky? *There was only one rational explanation,* he thought, *they were being followed, but by whom?* Falhinir leant against the side of the ferry and gazed at his rippled reflection in the water. Everything seemed so calm and peaceful. His mind drifted to thoughts of his family and how long it would be before he could see them again. He cast his mind back to that awful day when the Warriors attacked Romney. He had been busy working inside the farmhouse, his father and sisters tending to the sheep in the meadow outside. He would never forget the terror that consumed him at the moment he realised he was trapped inside. He could still smell the smoke and taste the soot and ash of his burning home. He had just caught a glimpse of one of the dreaded Warriors as it threw a burning torch to the thatched roof of the house. The evil yellow eyes of the beast paralysed him with fear...

Falhinir was startled as Sebastian placed his hand upon his shoulder, bringing him back to the present. Lost in his thoughts, it had not taken long for them to reach the opposite side of the river.

'How far do you think we will get today?' Falhinir asked Æthelwulf as they disembarked from the ferry.

'We have a good seven hours riding before nightfall,' replied the knight, 'I have family in St. Albans. We can stop there for a short rest and then head for Leicester. If we try and stay close to large cities, the Warriors may not be able to find us so easily. It should take about two hours to reach St. Albans from here.'

Falhinir looked over his shoulder at Arnor and Sebastian. 'We are going to St. Albans, Æthelwulf has family there, and we will be able to stop and rest before heading for Leicester.'

Arnor nodded in agreement. Sebastian however, was not entirely trusting of Æthelwulf although it was nothing he could put his finger on. The knight had been helpful and accommodating but the little man was not happy about the arrangement, there being no alternative plan on offer, he kept his misgivings to himself and they set off towards St Albans.

Chapter V

Æthelwulf's Haven

It was shortly after midday when the imposing red brick walls of the Abbey of St. Alban loomed upon the horizon. Around it had grown a thriving rural community. Once, the important Roman town of Verulamium; it was again becoming a noted centre of commerce. The main roman road of Watling Street ran directly through St Albans from London and had continued to be a well-travelled trading route with many inns and hostelries along the way to welcome the weary traveller. The once imposing roman walls that had encircled the old city were beginning to fall into ruin and in some places, the stone had all but disappeared, stolen by contemporary builders to be reused in new buildings around the city. The ramparts still looked foreboding though in the early afternoon gloom. Falhinir looked up and surveyed the grey sky above him. It looked as if it might rain and the thought of travelling to Leicester and getting wet and cold did not appeal to him, or he suspected the rest of the little band of travellers, in the slightest.

'Not far now,' Æthelwulf told the others as they walked their horses past the overhanging houses and through the narrow streets.

'We ought not stay too long, for it is not safe to do so with the Warriors after us, but good lord, I could do with a decent night's sleep' sighed a weary Sebastian, for the adventure had started to take its toll on him.

Falhinir agreed. 'We will only stay long enough to refresh the horses and ourselves. We have enough supplies to get us to Leicester.'

Æthelwulf led his companions to a small wooden cottage that stood adjacent to a rather welcoming looking inn called Ye Fighting Cocks. The cottage and the inn were directly in the shadow of the great Abbey. 'This is the home of my mother,' he said. The door creaked as he pushed it open. 'Mother?' he called out. From the darkness of an adjacent room appeared the small figure of a fragile looking oldishwoman. Barely five feet tall, she had long silver hair that just touched her shoulders, she looked frail but within her was an inner strength that would have made her formidable in her younger years. The pervading sunlight that shone through a small window revealed a face that had once been beautiful but that was now suffering the ravages of time. 'Æthelwulf?' she asked.

'Yes mother,' replied her son, taking her by the hand, 'I am sorry it has been so long.' He had not seen his mother since he had left for Kent several months before.

His mother gave him a loving smile. 'I am just so pleased to see you, and who are your friends? Come in from the cold and warm yourselves beside the fire. I don't have much in the house for your guests but we can fetch some mead and stew from yonder inn. I would have preferred to have been able to feed you by my own hand but with it only being me at home and you away, I don't have need of many provisions' her voice tailed off wistfully.

'Thank you, that will be marvellous' Arnor replied before she could get too melancholy. Æthelwulf pointed to his companions turn. 'Mother, this is Falhinir, Sebastian and Arnor.' He turned to his companions, 'This is my mother, May.'

'Are you staying long?' asked May, hope in her voice.

Falhinir stepped forward. 'No, I am afraid that we are just passing through. We are on our way to Leicester.' He said, not noticing the plea in her voice.

'I'll go and fetch the supplies,' said Æthelwulf as May invited the others to sit around the solid but well-worn oak table set in the centre of the room.

'What brings you here to St. Albans?' May asked, taking the jug of mead from Æthelwulf when he returned some minutes later. He had been gone longer that the others expected and his absence had created a slightly uncomfortable silence in the little cottage.

'We are on a journey of great importance,' said Falhinir slightly pompously, taking a cup of mead gratefully from May and swallowing the contents down in one gulp.

'Please, tell me more,' she replied, eyeing the jug of mead which she knew to be of the finest quality and probably stronger than the young man was used to.

Falhinir started to recount their journey so far and when the jug was empty, Arnor slipped out to replenish it from the alehouse next door. As the companions told their story, embellishing and interrupting with forgotten snippets, there came an urgent knocking at the cottage door. The companions looked at each other anxiously immediately jumping to the conclusion that the Warriors had caught up with them somehow. May went to open the door as the others surreptitiously palmed their weapons, ready to defend themselves in the small confined space between the door and the table if it became necessary.

'Good afternoon, mistress" came a reedy voice from behind the door 'We noticed that you have visitors, could it perchance be your son Æthelwulf?' The voice enquired politely. The seated travellers relaxed slightly, it was not in the nature of a Warrior to be polite, this was obviously someone else.

"It is indeed" exclaimed May, stepping aside for the visitor to enter.

"I am Pius, a messenger from the Abbey" revealed the stranger as he stood in the threshold. 'I have a message from the Abbot, your son and his fellow knight are to make haste to the Abbey. He is anxious to hear the outcome of their mission to Kent. There is also a message that needs to be conveyed to the king of Mercia, your presence here will save us having to arrange delivery by other means,' he gabbled. He was clearly slightly in awe of the well-armed men sat around the table. The two knights looked wearily at each other. They had wanted to come to St Albans without paying a visit to the Abbey, as was customary for visiting knights. They had clearly been spotted at they had entered the city walls and the old abbot, a notorious gossip, who liked nothing better than to live vicariously through the exploits of others, expected them to entertain him.

Arnor sighed "Thank you Pius, you may tell the Father that we shall be along to pay our respects to the abbey, within the hour.' The young friar nodded and made to take his leave.

"Come now, we can at least send you back to the Abbey with a drink for your trouble" offered Falhinir proffering a cup of mead. 'This really is excellent mead" he added sloshing the last of the jug into his own cup.

Once the young monk had been sent on his way, Arnor spoke "The abbot is likely to keep us up at the abbey all evening" he said 'It really is most inconvenient that we were seen as we entered the city, I think under the circumstances, it would be best to stay overnight so as to not raise suspicion as to our true purpose. We will be as safe here as out on the open road; besides, it has begun to rain and some of us…' his voice trailed off but he looked pointedly at the slightly swaying Falhinir.

Sebastian looked suspiciously at the two knights, trying to assess whether the invitation had been contrived to ambush them. He spoke slowly 'I think the boy and I will remain here until you return. We should try and keep a low profile. The less people that see us here, the better.'

Arnor nodded as he and Æthelwulf stood and made to leave for the Abbey.

Sebastian looked appraisingly at May, 'I'm sure we can find enough to occupy ourselves for a few hours' he joked.

"I'd better get some more mead' slurred Falhinir grabbing the jug and making his way slightly unsteadily towards the door.

Falhinir entered the dimly lit interior of the inn. His eyes took a few moments to adjust to change in light. He squinted towards the bar area and tried to focus. Behind the bar his eyes were assaulted by a vision of absolute loveliness. A girl of about his age was bent forward pulling foaming liquid into a bottle from a cask propped up in front of her. Her yellow hair, the colour of bright sunlight he mused, was escaping from under her cap as her upper body shuddered from the effort of drawing the ale. She was wearing a low-cut bodice and her bosoms were jiggling, most distractingly, with the effort. She had dancing brown eyes and a beaming smile.

"Be with you in a second" she spoke and Falhinir thought her words were the voices of angels. He just stood gazing stupidly at her, his ears going slightly pink.

'Mood gafternoon' he spluttered, "we mead more need". He waved the jug in her general direction whilst tripping up the step that was in front of the bar. The girl laughed and took the jug from him. He stood with his jaw hanging open as she went about filling it efficiently from the vat on the trestle behind her. Falhinir noticed there was much jiggling and giggling from the young girl as she went about her work. He thought he had never seen a lovelier, more beautiful girl in his entire life. She passed the jug back to Falhinir and moved off to serve another customer. He couldn't think of anything witty or useful to say to the lass so, crestfallen, he thanked her and slunk back to the cottage looking over his shoulder to catch a last glimpse of her.

He re-entered the cottage to find Sebastian and May chatting amiably by the fire. They had pulled a settle to the warmest spot and were sitting contentedly like an old married couple side by side. He set the mead on the table and poured himself a generous measure, the other two still had almost half a cup left each. The pair by the fire hardly noticed he was there, as they carried on their conversation. He sat and drank his cup of mead resentfully, excluded from their contented twosome. Watching the flames crackle and spit he began dreaming a daydream where he and the girl from the alehouse were running hand in hand through a wheat field. As he mused on his future with the girl, he continued to sip the cup. It was not that long before he was surprised to notice the jug was empty again.

'Mead, more" he mumbled as he rose unsteadily and made his way to the door. Sebastian looked at him distractedly, he was enjoying the companionship of a woman sitting beside an open fire. It had been many years since he had had the chance to do so. He was not about to go out in the rain and get wet, just for the sake of another drink. He had had sufficient to feel mellow and sleepy, he hadn't had that much to drink and he still had his wits about him. He assumed Falhinir was in the same condition, which was probably very far from the truth. The old man had many years of practice more than the boy had, in his capacity to drink but still, he let the boy go. He couldn't get into too much trouble walking next door and back, surely.

The tavern was a lot busier than when Falhinir had been in the first time. The girl behind the bar had been joined by an older heavier set man who took the jug from him and filled it before Falhinir could say anything. He paid the money and was just about to leave without engaging with the girl at all when he was distracted by a raucous crowd to his right.

"What's going on over there?" He asked no-one in particular. His mouth felt like it was full of stones and he had trouble getting the words out in the right order.

"That's the cock-pit" the girl replied as she squeezed past him returning empty bottles to the bar. "The what?' He repeated puzzled. "It's where the cock fights take place" she offered moving away. She really was the most beautiful creature had ever seen, he mooned.

Cock fights, he thought, that sounds more interesting than watching the old folks mouldering in front of the fire. He made his way over toward the noise and found himself on the edge of an octagonal enclosure surrounded on all sides by baying men. The edge was at elbow height but as he shoved his way to the wooden railing and peered over, he could see that the interior of the "ring" was several feet lower, pannelled and with sheer walls. The bottom of the pit was covered in a layer of lumpy sand which puzzled him slightly, why was it lumpy? Several men were shouting and waving money in the air. Two men at opposite sides of the ring were holding baskets aloft and yelling about how many wins they had achieved. Falhinir took a swig from the jug still clutched in his hand. He was getting caught up in the excitement of the shouting and waving. Just as he was wishing he had sufficient funds with him to place a bet, for that was what he realised all the men were doing, betting, there came a hush. The men clutching the baskets lowered them to the edge of the enclosure and a loud bell sounded. Both men released the catches on their baskets and the birds within were flung down into the bottom of the pit.

One was a cockerel with bright plumage and aggressive little black beady eyes. It had sharpened claws but had been made more menacing by the addition of silver points on his spurs. It looked formidable as it strutted round the bottom of the pit. The other bird was a slightly smaller and fatter brown gamecock with reinforcements on his spurs. He too had aggressive eyes although his were yellow and looked indignantly around as he surveyed his surroundings and his opponent. The assembled crowd began roaring and goading the two birds whilst shaking their fists and leaning over the railing so far, they were in danger of falling in. Falhinir could now see why it was lower on the inside than the outside. In a flurry of squawking and feathers the birds flew at each other with their spurs outstretched. They seemed intent on killing each other as soon as possible. First the bigger bird seemed to have the upper hand as the brown feathers became tinged with red as the vicious spurs inflicted wounds on the breast and back of the smaller cock. This seemed to enrage him further and he attacked his bigger opponent with an aggressive flurry of claws using his beak to peck at the eyes and wattle of the taller cockerel. After a few minutes of flurried attack, both birds were dripping blood from nasty wounds. The blood fell into the pit and was balled up by the sand. It was pretty gruesome to watch and Falhinir could see now why the sand was lumpy. *How many other birds had lost their fights this evening?* he wondered slightly queasily. The owner of the cockerel was whispering to the owner of the brown gamecock and leaned over and rang the bell again. It seemed the bout was over. The gamecock had won and the other bird was retrieved from the pit, injured but not fatally so. The onlookers were clearly disappointed, expecting a fight to the death, they felt cheated that the fight had been brought to a premature end. The owners withdrew from the edge of the arena and were replaced by another two, holding baskets aloft. Falhinir had been swigging from the mead jug during the contest and was feeling decidedly ebullient as the new combatants began shouting the odds and taking bets. Suddenly, he remembered the pouch of coins Arnor had given him following their strange swordfight. He was trying to remember where he had put them when he felt a hand on his shoulder. "Why, hello Sebastian" yelled Falhinir a little too loudly "Have you come to make a bet?" Sebastian could see that his eyes were somewhat out of focus and although the words had left Falhinir lucidly, they had arrived at Sebastian in a slurred drawl.

'Come 'ere, you bloody fool,' Sebastian growled under his breath, 'we are supposed to be keeping a low profile.' He grabbed the drunk lad by a handful of his tunic and began to manhandle him through the bar. The serving girl caught Falhinir's eye as he was frog marched from the premises. 'Isn't she gorgeous?' He drooled stupidly at Sebastian who just harrumphed and applied more vigour to getting the boy out of the tavern. The rain was falling gently as the fresh air hit the boy. As it did so Falhinir suddenly had an overwhelming urge to vomit. He pushed Sebastian from him but could not help splattering the little man's shoes as he re-visited the stew and mead that had been churning in his stomach.

‘Serves you right” muttered the little man, furious that there was sick on his shoes but aware that the boy would feel better tomorrow if he had emptied his stomach. “Come on, let’s get you to bed” he said gently. “You’re going to feel awful tomorrow’

When the boy had steadied himself and wiped the last of the vomit from his mouth, the unlikely pair staggered the few yards from the inn to the cottage. May was nowhere to be seen and the fire had been banked up for the night. Sebastian deposited the practically unconscious lad on the settle and covered him with a rough woollen blanket. He was asleep within seconds and was snoring loudly as Sebastian blew out the tallow candle that was the only thing lighting the room barring the fire. The rain persisted into the night but the occupants of the cottage were unaware of conditions outside as they settled in for the night.

The knights arrived from the Abbey after they had breakfasted with Father Abbot. He had kept his side of the bargain and they had dined well at his table and chosen to stay the night at the abbey in rudimentary monks' quarters, rather than venturing out into the cold and wet late into the evening. They had prayed with the Abbot at dawn and were rearing to hit the road as they arrived at the cottage. Falhinir was still snoring loudly in front of the embers of the fire and Sebastian, on hearing their approaching conversation, had sheepishly opened the door from May's bedchamber and was making a big show of cleaning his shoes as the two knights entered the living room.

Falhinir woke with a thumping headache and was feeling distinctly sorry for himself as they made preparations to leave. May had appeared with cheese and bread for breakfast and whilst she and Sebastian ate heartily, Falhinir couldn't face a thing. 'Here lad, get this down you' Sebastian said sympathetically, he offered a chunk of dry bread 'you'll feel better with something inside you' he said kindly. Falhinir, took the bread and tried to swallow some, wondering what had put the little man in such a good mood this morning.

After breakfast, Sebastian peered out of the window and noticed that the sun had begun to rise further into the sky. 'I am afraid we will have to be going very shortly. The day is moving on and we have many hours' travel ahead of us,' he declared.

The others acknowledged this and finished whatever food and drink they had remaining. Sebastian, Arnor and Falhinir thanked their host for everything she had done for them. May accompanied her guests to the narrow street outside her house where they reluctantly mounted their horses. They had enjoyed the warmth of the welcome the little cottage had afforded them. St Albans had provided a brief respite from the perils of their journey, even if the mead had been too much for poor Falhinir, He was still feeling distinctly unwell with a pounding headache he just couldn't shift. He mounted his horse unsteadily and noticed his hands were shaking.

Outside the adjacent tavern there was a young girl of about Falhinir's age. She had a bony body and slight squint. She looked in the direction of the greenish looking Falhinir as she poured a couple of buckets of rainwater on what appears to be a pile of slops on the ground in front of the tavern.

'Bloody drunks' she muttered under her breath, she had several teeth missing and it came out with a slight whistle. She beamed at Falhinir with a gummy smile. 'Hello, again" she said. Falhinir ignored her and turned away.

'What an ugly looking wench' he whispered to Sebastien who just smirked, thinking to himself that they should be grateful that the stupid boy was far too drunk the night before to have taken his alcoholic infatuation any further. They had enough problems without being pursued by angry fathers protecting their daughter's virtue. Still, thought Sebastien, it was yet one more thing the old man had to worry about. They could well do without romantic attachments on this trip.

As Æthelwulf was saying good bye to his mother, Falhinir noticed her giving him something wrapped in a piece of cloth. He thought it strange that Æthelwulf was quick to conceal the item, but he soon turned his mind to the journey ahead.

As the companions rode away from St. Albans, Falhinir attempted to distract himself from his general malaise by turning his attention to the concerns Sebastian had expressed about Æthelwulf. 'Do you still think he is not to be trusted?' Falhinir asked.

'I'll admit that I might be wrong about him,' he replied. However, there was something still bothering him. He couldn't articulate what it was exactly but it was there nonetheless and Sebastian always trusted his instincts. 'His mother has a familiarity about her though.' He mused, 'It seemed to me, I have come across her before somewhere, some place long ago.' His voice sounded as if he was remembering something from a faraway place. Falhinir gave Sebastian a look suggesting that the old man had perhaps had more mead than was good for him. He was obviously sensitive to the effects the mead could have on your general constitution and wellbeing. He thought it probable the little man had been as drunk as he had been, conveniently forgetting the small matter of being dragged from the inn and throwing up all over Sebastian's shoes. 'I don't believe you sometimes, how could you possibly know her?' he asked with a superior chuckle.

'I don't know, but I am sure that I have seen her somewhere before.'

Sensing his friend was about to launch into one of his tall tales, Falhinir rode on ahead to catch up with Arnor and Æthelwulf, leaving Sebastian alone with his fanciful notions as to why it was that May had seemed so familiar to him.

The sun was low on the

horizon as they approached the Great Ouse. When they arrived, the four friends found that the only means of crossing was by way of a lonely ferry. On the far side they could see an area of dense woodland, and they agreed that it was a safe enough shelter for the night.

Once they were all aboard the ferry, Falhinir turned and looked back across the landscape they had just travelled. *There is someone out there following us*, he thought. He knew it would be too much to expect to maybe catch a glimpse of whoever it might be as he stared across the fields. He had to find a way of catching their pursuer, but in any case, it was getting dark and any further speculation would do well to wait until the morning.

As dusk fell, the cold night air became damp and heavy. The four friends huddled around a small fire that afforded little warmth. Each one was alone with their thoughts and the memory of the cosy cottage they had left in St Albans as they shuffled around trying to get comfortable on the hard ground.

'We had better get some rest,' said Arnor, wrapping his cloak more tightly around himself.

'How far is it to the Forest Lands from here?' Falhinir asked Æthelwulf, ignoring Sebastian's heavy snoring. That man could sleep anywhere, he thought

'Four days' journey to the north,' he replied, 'we would do well to stay here tonight, and hope that we do not meet any of those Warriors.'

'Let's hope not,' Falhinir replied as he and his companions settled down for the night.

Chapter VI
Lost Causes

Dawn had just broken when Sebastian was woken by a dewdrop landing squarely in the middle of his forehead. It was cold and rather unpleasantly lumpy laying on the ground under some tall trees. They had afforded some protection from the rain that had fallen during the night but not nearly enough. He yelped as the damp splat assaulted his senses awake and sat up. The others were already stirring from their slumbers and so he began to rise and arrange himself for the day ahead.

Arnor looked at Falhinir. 'Long day's riding today,' he said, running his fingers through his long hair, 'I hope you are feeling up to it, you were definitely a little off colour yesterday'

'Oh, don't worry, I am feeling much better today' replied the boy with a yawn, stretching his arms out behind his head. If the effects of his overindulgence had indeed worn off, there was more than enough for him to worry about besides that. Despite his assurances that he was raring to go, Falhinir was far from looking forward to once again embarking upon his journey. He grew more and more uncertain with every step that brought him closer to Ceridwen and her troublesome book.

'Looks like you are!' Sebastian said sarcastically. 'Where's Æthelwulf?' he continued, looking around. Arnor and Falhinir looked at each other and shrugged their shoulders. Sebastian got up, walked over to Falhinir and crouched down beside him. 'I told you he was not to be trusted. Do you still have the map? Where are the horses? I told you! I told you he was...' Sebastian had started on what could have been a lengthy rant when he was interrupted by a voice behind him.

'You told him I was what?' called out the voice. Sebastian spun round to find himself looking into the eyes of Æthelwulf himself. He had emerged from a thicket of undergrowth but had clearly heard the little man voicing his opinion to the others.

'Err, err...' stuttered Sebastian, not really sure what he had heard and certainly not wanting to repeat the slurs to the bigger man.

'I see you had gone to find something to eat,' Falhinir interjected, trying to avoid leaving Sebastian floundering with what to say. Æthelwulf stomped over to where Sebastian was stood, looked him squarely in the eye and dropped two dead rabbits at his feet. 'I'll get the fire ready,' Æthelwulf told Falhinir, his cold gaze still fixed on Sebastian's back. The little man made a big show of preparing the rabbits for the pot but had you looked closely at Sebastian you would have been able to see that he still looked worried.

Soon after they had eaten their somewhat tense breakfast, they set off riding across the fields of Middle Anglia, each field and settlement they passed taking them closer to their mysterious destination. After they had been riding for several hours, Falhinir was beginning to get a little saddle weary and was hoping for the chance soon to dismount and stretch his legs. He knew that there was a fair way to go before nightfall. They did not want to sleep on the roadside any more than was necessary. Not with the Warriors close on their heels. They had come within earshot of loud screaming and shouting carrying on the breeze. Bringing their horses to a slow walk, they each cast about the surrounding countryside with their eyes trying to pinpoint the direction and source of the commotion.

'Over there!' shouted Arnor, pointing towards thick plumes of smoke a little way off into the distance.

'What on earth could it be?' Falhinir asked the others, fearing another village was being attacked by the Warriors. His mind was immediately taken back to that fateful night on Romney Marsh when this dreadful adventure had begun. He dragged his mind away from the images that lurked so closely behind his eyes and focused on what was in front of him.

'A lost cause,' replied Æthelwulf. 'The four Kingdoms of Middle Anglia, Deira, Lindsey and Mercia are constantly fighting. Each of the Kingdoms lays claim to the lands of their neighbours. They have been in this state of constant fighting for many years. Only when this island is truly united, will there be lasting peace between all the Kingdoms. Only under one strong leader can we have stability.'

Arnor leant into Æthelwulf's ear. 'I wonder what King Æthelred would think if he heard you say that?' he whispered.

Æthelwulf did not reply.

'Can we go around the battle?' Falhinir asked Arnor.

'It'll take too long to go around it completely, we can do our best to avoid it but we have to go quite close' he replied, 'The trail to the Forest Lands takes us in that direction. We should just keep moving and try to maintain a safe distance.' With that, they gingerly made their way forward towards the sounds of the battle in progress before them. They hadn't travelled much further before they found themselves on a hilltop, overlooking the smouldering remains of a small town. Again, Falhinir was reminded of the terrible day the Warriors destroyed his own settlement. Falhinir, again, tried to push his thoughts away but this time they were too close to the surface. He felt a pang of sadness as his memories came flooding back to him; the smoke, the fire, death and carnage. He felt he could still smell the smoke and taste the burning wood as a relentless torrent of flames engulfed his home...... It was much more likely to be the effects of the battle joined beneath their vantage point, the echo of men's voices releasing him from the past. A hundred or so paces away there was a full battle raging with more than a thousand soldiers engaged in combat.

'Can you tell who it is Æthelwulf?' asked Arnor.

'Those are the colours of Ecgferth of Deira Æthelwulf squinted down at the throng for a moment, attempting to make out the colours of the opposing combatants. 'Oh bugger! Arnor, it's Æthelred!' Æthelwulf looked aghast at his companion, his eyes wide. Without a moment's hesitation, there passed between the two men an understanding. They were Æthelred's men, there was no question.

Arnor turned to Falhinir. 'We have to go down there but for your own protection it would be better if you stayed up here, you should be safe enough this far away.'

A dark angry look flushed across Falhinir's face. 'I'm coming with you!' he exclaimed. He had a twofold reason for following the two knights into the battle. The first was that, naturally, he wanted the chance to help his friends but secondly and, in his opinion, more importantly, he was not going to be robbed of the chance to engage in real combat for the first time.

'Don't be a bloody fool boy!' Arnor shouted back looking angry himself. 'There is too much at stake. You are in enough danger as it is. Do not risk your life unnecessarily! We have no choice but to assist our King. If he was to learn that we were here and did not offer our service, he will have us executed! You have a much higher purpose to fulfil. We cannot allow you to get killed in such an unnecessary skirmish as this'

Falhinir looked at Sebastian for some sort of affirmation or back up to his desire to satisfy his bloodlust but was met with the old man shaking his head, his mouth set firm.

'Listen to him Falhinir,' Sebastian countered calmly before the boy could make his appeal. At that moment Falhinir knew he was not going to win the argument no matter how much he protested. He was just wasting time and preventing the other two from joining their King.

'Alright, I'll stay here!' he sulked like a small child.

'Make sure he doesn't do anything foolish!' Æthelwulf yelled over his shoulder toward Sebastian as he and Arnor dug their horses in the flanks and sped off towards the battle.

As Arnor and Æthelwulf thundered

down the hillside on their heavy steeds, they realised that Æthelred had suffered a great deal of losses even before they had arrived. Their King was being encircled for his own protection and surrounded by a pitifully small number of his remaining men on horseback. The two knights charged as fast as they could in the general direction of their King and his depleted band of allies.

'My Lord!' shouted Æthelwulf anxious to ensure that their King knew that they were there, in the thick of the action.

Æthelred acknowledged the pair with a weary nod. Arnor looked at Æthelwulf and drew his sword and raised it above his head Æthelwulf did the same and they turned towards their enemy and plunged into the middle of the battle, slashing and thrusting into the soft fleshy parts of the enemy on foot in front of them. The superior swords and heavy hooves made short work of the foot soldiers in front of them. They were completely outnumbered, though and could only do so much to hold back the relentless tide of their enemy, protect their King and save the remnants of his army.

Meanwhile, up on the hill, Falhinir could see what was happening and was becoming increasingly agitated. 'We must help them Sebastian!' he shouted.

'It is not our fight. Do not get involved!' Sebastian told Falhinir sternly. 'If something should happen to you, what would happen then? There will be no one to challenge Tuan and his army. You must not be so reckless.'

Falhinir fidgeted on his horse. 'I just can't sit here and watch our friends risk their lives, I have to do something!' He pleaded

Sebastian pondered for a moment. 'Perhaps there is something we can do. I have an idea, follow me!' he exclaimed as he flung himself from his horse, grabbed his bag and ran pell mell down the grassy bank.

Falhinir secured the horses and followed him down the hill as he lunged into an area of long grass that bordered the edge of the battlefield, Falhinir flung himself down just as Sebastian took his bow and quiver slung over his back. Falhinir did the same and with deadly accuracy the pair of them set to firing into the mass of archers that were gathered beneath Ecgferth's banners. They had succeeded in killing several of Ecgferth's men but it wasn't going to be enough to turn the tide of the battle. Peering through the tall grass, they could see Æthelred's depleted army retreating into the distance, being chased eagerly by a few of Ecgferth's men. As the battlefield emptied of Æthelred's army it became clear to both Falhinir and Sebastian that Ecgferth's forces had several prisoners under guard. They searched the faces of the weary prisoners but could not find their friends amongst the crestfallen faces.

Æthelwulf and Arnor, had seen their King departing the battlefield and having acknowledged them on the field, knew he would not be bothered about their whereabouts for now. For all Æthelred knew, they could have been taken prisoner. To ensure that they avoided capture they escaped the fighting and returned to the hilltop. They found Falhinir and Sebastian's horses unattended and no sign of the pair of them 'Where the hell are they?' Arnor exclaimed in a rare emotional outburst. 'They were told to remain here'

'Look!' Æthelwulf cried, pointing down the hill. From their elevated vantage point, he had spotted their companions lying in the grass. A small group of enemy soldiers were advancing toward them but not anticipating anyone being in this area they were not moving with any stealth.

Falhinir and Sebastian thought that perhaps it wasn't a good idea to hang around and wait to be captured by these troops. As Ecgferth's forces had begun to clear the battlefield and looked like they were going to be around for quite a while, both of them realised that they could soon be trapped in their thicket of grass. 'Do you think we will get back up the hill unnoticed?' Falhinir whispered to Sebastian.

'Follow me,' his friend whispered in return, 'we are going to have to move silently and very quickly. Are you ready?'

Falhinir nodded in acknowledgement.

Sebastian had to wait until the soldiers that were nearby decided to return to the battlefield and the looting of the enemy corpses. He knew that they wouldn't be able to stay away from them and as soon as they were sufficiently far away 'Right, go!' he shouted, and with that he and Falhinir began make their hasty ascent of the hill.

They had to climb the hill from a different angle to keep out of sight as much as possible. They were relying on the looting to keep their enemies' eyes focused elsewhere. Being quite a steep hill, it wasn't easy for the ageing Sebastian to keep up with his young friend who shot up the grassy knoll like a jackrabbit. It had taken poor Sebastian a good ten minutes to get just over half way to the top. Sebastian had forgotten how tiring it was climbing up steep slopes, remembering fleetingly, dashing up and down the rough grassy escarpments above the Romney Marsh near

Lympne when he was a boy. Looking up, they could see Arnor and Æthelwulf peering down at them, and he attempted to pick up their pace a bit. 'I'm getting too old for all this' thought Sebastian as an unseen rabbit hole caught his foot and twisted his ankle. Needless to say, he fell. Laying spread eagle on his front, he slipped back down the slope on the damp grass. His progress was hindered by the various shrubs and small trees that littered the hillside, but it was not enough to stop him, and he landed heavily back amongst the long grass where he had started. Falhinir could see Arnor and Æthelwulf waving to him, beckoning him to carry on up the hill, but Falhinir didn't think twice about turning tail and chasing down the hill after his friend.

Of course, the soldiers down below could hardly fail to miss such a spectacle, Sebastian had accompanied his descent with his usual and not subtle litany of curses and swearwords that had caused the soldiers to stop their looting and see what all the noise was about. On seeing a little chubby man sliding down the hill followed by a waving youth they thought they had better go and investigate. By the time Falhinir had reached Sebastian they were surrounded by half a dozen Deiran soldiers, pointing swords and arrows at them. Falhinir and Sebastian had little choice but to reluctantly hand over their weapons and raise their hands in surrender.

'Damn it!' exclaimed Arnor. 'They're being led off; we'll have to follow.'

Æthelwulf and Arnor could only watch helplessly as the prisoners were piled onto the back of a wagon, which eventually lumbered away deeper into the countryside.

It was late in the afternoon when Falhinir and Sebastian realised they were close to their destination. An old Roman fort began to emerge as they lurched towards the brow of another hill. This fortress, like many others, had fallen to Ecgferth during a sustained campaign of the Middle Lands. The Saxons had originally believed Roman ruins to be haunted but many years of war and the need for secure places for prisoners had long surpassed any lingering superstition or fear.

Following behind by some quarter of a mile were Arnor and Æthelwulf. 'They must be getting close to their camp by now, we have travelled at least fifteen miles,' said Æthelwulf. He was becoming frustrated that his friends were in this predicament. 'Had they not decided to try and help us out in the battle, they would never had been captured' he lamented. Arnor placed his hand on Æthelwulf's arm and pointed to the fort in the distance. 'If they go in there, we will never get them out,' he sighed.

Falhinir and Sebastian looked at each other pensively as they approached the foreboding building. It was obvious that Ecgferth had won the campaign of the Middle Lands and was going to be around for a very long time. The menacing turrets reached far into the sky, where buzzards were circling above the battlements, scavenging on the remains of men abandoned up there as they so often did. To Falhinir and Sebastian they were a most unwelcome addition to this troubled landscape. As the wagon drew ever closer, the dark stone walls gave a stronger and stronger impression of being impenetrable.

'Open the gates, we have the prisoners!' shouted one of the mounted soldiers, and the massive wooden gates opened, as if they were the jaws of some great stone beast. The wagon proceeded inside. Looking at their new surroundings from the back of the wagon, Falhinir and Sebastian realised they had arrived at a garrison; a large one by the look of it. The wagon had pulled up in an open courtyard where many men were busy at work. They were blacksmiths mostly, producing weapons and armour for Ecgferth's unforgiving war machine. Falhinir did not feel that any chance of rescue or escape was in their favour in the least. He was suddenly startled and Sebastian jumped as a loud thud signalled the great wooden doors behind them were shut. The strangely solid sound echoed throughout the courtyard. They were left in no doubt that, for them, there was no escape.

Æthelwulf stared at the castle as he watched the wagon disappear through the gates.

'How far are Æthelred's soldiers from here?' asked Arnor.

'Eight, maybe ten miles southwest,' replied Æthelwulf. 'There are not enough of us to siege the castle, look at the place, not even Æthelred's home is this mighty.'

'I wasn't thinking about a siege,' said Arnor, 'many of Æthelred's knights are men of these lands, maybe one of them knows of this place and what its weaknesses are.'

Æthelwulf looked at Arnor. 'Only one way to find out, do you think we will find the army before dusk? I don't want to be out on the trail with Ecgferth's still looking for stragglers. Not in this get up' he glanced meaningfully at his tunic bearing the colours of the defeated army.

'It won't make much difference,' Arnor replied, 'if we have any chance of saving them it will have to be done under the cover of darkness.'

They turned and rode off across the countryside in search of their King.

Falhinir, Sebastian and the other prisoners were herded off the wagon and assembled in the courtyard. A large bearded man seemed to be in charge. They were not left hanging around for long before the armed guards were galvanised into action. 'Take them below!' Beardy ordered, and the captured men were ushered into the darkness of the fort.

Led by torchlight, they followed a soldier down a series of tunnels that twisted and turned into the depths of the earth. They seemed to be in a network of subterranean fissures and caves that had been hewn deep beneath the fortress.

'What will they do, kill us?' Falhinir asked Sebastian in a nervous whisper.

'If they wanted to do that, they would have done it already,' Sebastian replied.

No communication, keep quiet all of

you!' yelled one of the guards.

The group were corralled into a smaller cavern and individually shackled to the walls, the remains of the previous occupants were scattered all about them in various states of decay. The stench hung in air as Falhinir and Sebastian glanced at each other nervously. Gradually, the light from the soldier's torches receded and they were plunged into total darkness.

Light was fading fast as Æthelwulf and Arnor continued to traverse the surrounding terrain in search of their King and his army. Eventually after many hours, they finally tracked them down to a small farming settlement. They discovered that Æthelred was holed up within one of the nearby farmhouses, recovering, before making a run for the border and the relative safety of his own lands.

The two knights hitched their horses to a rickety fence surrounding the property, walked around to the front and boldly knocked on the door. It was answered by a couple of wary looking young guards who were clearly expecting more hostile visitors. Upon realising who they were, the knights were ushered quickly inside and led into a small chamber that had been commandeered as the private quarters of the King himself. Arnor and Æthelwulf stood before him and bowed their heads in respect.

'My friends!' he exclaimed as he shook them each by the hand, a trembling hand. A detail not unnoticed by the two visitors. His complexion was pale and he was sweating rather more than was healthy. He appeared as though he had not slept for days, his clothes were worn and dirty and his hair long. Æthelred's gaunt features were masked by an unkempt beard and his eyes looked hollow in his skull. A once handsome man had evolved into this tired and diminished creature before them. It was clear that today's battle was not his first recent defeat.

Having greeted these two of his most trusted soldiers, he turned and began pacing up and down, wringing his hands and mumbling to himself. Today he had experienced his most wounding defeat to date. The minor skirmishes that had led up to the recent battle had been damaging but nothing like on the scale of the losses he had endured today. The proud man was profoundly shaken by the experience. He sat down and stared vacantly out of a small window. 'What news do you have you from Kent?' he asked desperately seeking comforting news.

'King Ecgbryht has agreed to your offer and his troops are on way here as we speak,' replied Arnor hoping to comfort the King with his words.

'At least that is something,' replied the King, looking rather relieved. He pondered for a short while before continuing. 'You both fought bravely today,' he said, his voice trembling. 'Thank you.'

Arnor stepped forward and swallowed. 'We have news of the prisoners, Sire.'

'They are being held in a fort, eleven miles northeast of here,' added Æthelwulf.

Æthelred placed his palms together and

raised his hands to his lips, as though he were engaged in prayer. 'So, Ecgferth seeks to offer us a trade,' he muttered to himself.

'Trade?' asked Æthelwulf.

The King turned and looked at them both. 'Yes, we have many prisoners of theirs too. They were captured just outside of York, about a month ago. His brother Aldfrith is amongst them and he will be seeking to negotiate for his release.'

'We may have discovered another way. One that would put you at a considerable advantage in that regard' said Æthelwulf, after a short pause.

'Oh, how?' asked the King, raising his eyebrows, not sure how the balance of power could be turned in his favour.

Æthelwulf continued, ignoring the King's scepticism, 'Sire, as a good and fair leader, you have welcomed many men of these lands into your forces. Perhaps one amongst them is acquainted with this particular fortress and possibly a means of entering it unnoticed. It looks heavily fortified, but perhaps there is a weakness that can be exploited to our advantage.'

'I do not have nearly enough men here to attack a fort!' Æthelred exclaimed. He had attempted to capture a similar fortress some months before and had lost a large number of men. He did not want to deplete his forces any more by repeating the mistake.

'No, you don't,' replied Æthelwulf placatingly 'but perhaps there is a way that Arnor and myself, a small force, could gain access to the fortress by subterfuge and free our men. We do not have enough time to wait for Ecgferth's men to get here from York for the trade. He will start torturing and killing the prisoners if we do not act soon and we cannot afford to lose any more of our troops whilst we wait.' Arnor thought of something else as they sought to convince his monarch of their plan 'Once tortured, the men will tell him where his brother is being held, and you will then have to fight a war on two fronts,' Arnor added sagely. Æthelred pondered silently for a moment, there was a great deal of merit in their words. He spoke slowly 'There are two men who recently entered my service; they were brought up not far from here, they may know the fort of which you speak. Talk to them, find out what you can and report back to me.'

Arnor and Æthelwulf nodded in agreement and hurried away in search of the two recently recruited soldiers.

About an hour had passed before Arnor and Æthelwulf returned to the King's quarters accompanied by the two men. They were farmers, Gwion and Morvran, who had lost their lands to the Dierans during an earlier campaign and had decided to throw their lot in with Æthelred in the hope of exacting revenge.

'We have news, my Lord,' Arnor reported, 'we have found the soldiers, and they have informed us that there might be a way into the fortress.'

Gwion stepped forward and bowed his head. 'Sire, there are many caverns deep beneath the fortress that run far into the hills that surround us, there is also a path that leads into the farthest reaches of the caves beneath the fort. We have played in these tunnels and caves when we were children, when the Roman's had retreated. We know some of the routes but there is not a man alive who has complete knowledge of that place.

'Beware!' added Morvran, 'It is said that shortly after the Romans abandoned the fort at Midgard it was occupied by an evil sorcerer named Landraar. Local folklore tells that he performed terrible acts within those caves. There are many hidden dangers and unknown terrors that languish within the darkness of that place.'

Gwion glanced at each of the men around him and shuddered, 'This is a land of deep legend and myth. There are terrible and dangerous forces lurking here. Many men are aware of the legends but few will allow them to be mentioned, let alone discussed. A wise man would be mindful of these things at all times.'

'Can you prepare a chart that will show us the way through these caverns?' asked

Æthelwulf.

'Better than that,' Gwion interjected, 'we will have to show you. You have absolutely no chance of getting into and, crucially, out of, that fort, without our help.'

'Very well, Morvran, ready the horses,' Arnor ordered, 'we have not a moment to lose, we move tonight.'

As the small party was preparing to leave, a thought occurred to the King. He asked Arnor and Æthelwulf to wait behind in his chambers as the others departed. 'I am wondering,' he said, tapping his fingers whilst gazing out of the window at the brooding sky. 'You have not told me why it is so important that you rescue the prisoners tonight. If Ecgferth wants his brother back so desperately, surely he would be prepared to wait until he and the others are brought from York?'

Æthelwulf and Arnor looked at each other pensively, weighing up the consequences of revealing their true motives. It was one thing to be keeping secret the identity of the prisoners but there was also the small matter of the book. After all, the book had been the subject of great interest for many centuries. Most men would do anything to possess the knowledge contained within it. That would certainly give their king a battle advantage.

'Is there something I should be made aware of?' the King asked suspiciously noticing the reluctance of the knights to speak 'something you learned whilst on your duties in the south perhaps?'

Arnor took a deep breath and sighed 'The truth is, two of the prisoners are friends of ours. You are right, they are from the south. A place called the Romney Marsh to be precise. It is a strange place, very flat and bleak. It is not a place where one would wish to linger long. They have nothing to do with what is going on here, but it is imperative that they are not harmed.'

Æthelred looked at them thoughtfully, his eyes narrowed. 'Continue,' he said.

'They are on a great quest to save these lands,' Arnor continued with a flourish.

'Save these lands, from what, or who?'

asked the King, slightly intrigued, but also confused by the intoning timbre of Arnor's words. He was, he thought, the only person who could save Britain from the current tyranny.

'In a word, evil,' Æthelwulf interjected, 'an evil that has overshadowed these islands for a great many years, If the two of whom we speak, should fail, there is not a man woman or child in the entire land who will be safe.'

The King found the enormity of the pronouncement difficult to comprehend. 'What is this evil that you speak of?'

'It is an evil that had plagued these lands for centuries!' A voice from a dark recess cried out. 'It is that of an ancient Pagan, whose name I shall not utter.' From the shadows stepped a hooded figure who had been there all along but had only now made his presence felt. 'I feel his power growing, it burns within my soul,' said the aged voice from within the cloak. He pulled back his hood to reveal the stubbly face of an old man of around seventy years of age. His features were partly obscured by straggly white hair that ran past his shoulders but his gait as he emerged into the light was that of a much younger man. With his eyes closed, he approached the two knights. His feet shuffled along, as though feeling the ground as he walked towards them. The two knights found themselves startled as he lifted his eyelids. The old man was blind. He stared vacantly toward them with his opaque soulless eyes.

'Who are you?' asked Æthelwulf.

'This is my seer, Braantoch,' said the King, 'I have been seeking his council over today's defeat.'

Braantoch stood before Arnor and Æthelwulf, and after a short pause he spoke faintly; 'The boy and the old man who accompanies him must not be stopped from their journey. They must be allowed to continue. I know the one they seek. The one who will help them destroy the evil.' He extended a withered arm, stretched out his thin bony fingers and placed them upon Æthelwulf's chest. He paused for a second and withdrew his hand, muttering quietly to himself. He then turned to Arnor, stretching out his arm again, the old man placed his hand lightly upon the old knight's chest. As soon as his fingers came into contact with Arnor's tunic, Braantoch suddenly became very pale and began to tremble. Desperately he tried to speak but the words kept getting caught in his throat and he could not make a sound. Stumbling backward, he collapsed onto a stool, clutching his throat, his chest heaving as he sought to get his breathing under control. Æthelred rushed to his aid startled at what he had just witnessed. He was satisfied now that the two knights were acting honourably. 'Go now,' said the King, 'It seems to be important that you help your friends and my men.'

The knights left to prepare themselves for the evening's events. Braantoch started gently rocking on the spot as he watched them leave, repeating to himself:

'Non Omnis Moriar'
'Non Omnis Moriar'
'Non Omnis Moriar'
'Non Omnis Moriar'

Æthelred could only look on confused as Braantoch continued his mysterious chant. Although the old man was blind, Æthelred thought he could see terror in the old man's eyes. He took his hand to comfort him and as he did so he felt something damp in Braantoch's palm.

Upon closer inspection, he realised old man's hand was bleeding. There was a fresh wound. A wound in the form of a mysterious symbol.

Chapter VII
The
Caverns of Landraar

Dark thunderclouds rumbled angrily as torrents of rain poured in sheets upon the lonely hills of the moor. The strong wind battered the barren landscape as its mournful cry echoed through the darkness of the labyrinth deep beneath the fort.

Falhinir shivered in his chains as the eerie sounds that whispered around the caves crept into his ears. He had no idea of time or how long they had been down in the cave. All he did know is that he was beginning to get uncomfortable in his shackles. The ground was damp and cold and his bottom was numb from being in the same position. The pervading darkness of the cave was beginning to play on his mind too. He kept imagining what was hidden in the darkness and several times, he thought he felt something brush past him causing him to jump. This only caused greater pressure on his shackled limbs making the skin raw and painful. At the sound of distant movement, he strained his eyes towards what he thought was the direction of the passageway. There were definite signs that someone or something was coming toward the prisoners. The trouble with total darkness was that your imagination could play tricks on you, he mused. No, it was definitely signs of light, there was at least one torch coming down the passage from the fort above. He watched the light as it was joined by at least two others. "This cannot be good" he said to no-one in particular.

The guards advanced into the cave and lit the torches in their sconces above where the prisoners were shackled. They started examining the faces of each of their captives in turn. It was as though they were looking for someone in particular. With the addition of light in the cave. The captured army had begun to look around at themselves and a few of the prisoners began hailing their comrades from across the cave.

'Who are you?' asked the captured soldier immediately to the right of Sebastian, looking at Falhinir. 'I don't recognise you as part of our army.'

'We are friends of the knights Arnor and Æthelwulf,' interrupted Sebastian eagerly, 'we were captured after the battle and ...'

'You two!' yelled an authoritative voice, startling all the prisoners into silence.

Sebastian had been interrupted by one of the senior guards who had overheard the conversation. He was clearly looking straight at them. The pair looked at each other apprehensively. The guard who had spoken gestured at two other guards. They then came over to where they were sat and released Falhinir and Sebastian from their shackles. 'You're coming with us!' the senior guard intoned decisively.

'Where to?' asked Sebastian nervously.

'Be quiet and follow me!' the guard shouted in reply. Silently, they followed their captors into the dank corridors of the fort and away from the rest of the prisoners.

'How much further do we have to go?' Æthelwulf asked Morvran, having to shout over the relentless rain and thunder that pervaded the area in every direction.

'Not far now, the entrance is on the other side of the hill,' he replied in an equally loud voice. His words being carried away on the wind as soon as they left his mouth.

'Good!' exclaimed Arnor. 'I just want to get out of this bloody rain!'

Arnor and Æthelwulf followed Gwion and Morvran over a hill, their horses missing their footing and slipping down the muddy slope. They were now in the lee of the storm but the relentless rain beat down from above. 'This is it,' said Gwion as he led the two knights to a huge unnatural-looking crevice that ran deep into the hillside.

The two knights found themselves confronted by an ancient stone structure adorned with indecipherable images. It had been hewn from the natural rock but the stone working had caused the edifice to look alien and imposing on the natural landscape of the hillside. This was not what the knights were expecting as a "secret" entrance to the cave system. It was much too obvious and, well, visible. 'What is it?' asked Arnor.

'An ancient tomb,' replied Morvran, 'This entrance is man-made, but the chamber itself is natural. There is a well-hidden passageway on the far side of the interior that leads into the many caverns beneath Midgard. We are about a mile away from the fort itself but it is the only way to gain entry undetected.' He added. The entrance to the tomb actually formed part of a prehistoric burial mound that had been constructed using the natural formation of stone within the hillside.

Gwion reached into a bag and pulled from it a torch. He made to light it but had trouble getting it to burn in the entrance of the tomb. His tinder had got wet and it was difficult to get a decent spark from his flint. The others dismounted and stood in the entrance of the burial mound, sheltered from the wind and rain, Gwion was making heavy work of lighting the torch so Morvan took his own flint from within his tunic and lit the torch for him.

Together, the four approached the darkness of the void. As they crossed the threshold, Arnor and Æthelwulf looked about them and realised that they were standing in the entrance of, what appeared to be, a rather long corridor. They slowly walked onwards into the darkness noticing chambers had been created either side of the tomb as they went. Constructed using huge boulders, the tombs inside these chambers were filled with vast numbers of dis-articulated bones. Bones that had lain undisturbed for maybe, thousands of years. Arnor and Æthelwulf had seen many ancient sights on their long travels, including the standing stones in the south. Never before had they seen anything as unusual, or ancient, as this. They both remained silent, in awe of their surroundings, as they followed their guides deeper into the tomb.

'Stay close to the light' Morvan warned 'We still have quite a distance to walk before we reach the depths of the fortress'

'This is a treacherous path that we tread,' Gwion added 'Be very wary of the dangers that inhabit the darkness.' With that, he disappeared into a gap behind an enormous boulder. It was impossible to see the gap between the boulder and the wall of the cavern unless you knew it was there. This must be the entrance into the caves, thought Arnor and without another word they followed the two farmers into the darkness beyond.

Falhinir and Sebastian had followed the guard out of the passageways beneath the fortress and across the open courtyard where they had first arrived. It had started to get dark and rolling black clouds were threatening rain. The guards had been met by the bearded soldier who was clearly in charge of the prisoners. Beardy had taken over from the others and prodded Falhinir and Sebastian across the courtyard to a vast wooden door. He opened the door and shoved the captives inside in front of him. They were ushered into a vast wooden beamed hall. The room was dark and cold, scarcely benefiting from the light and heat of a large open fire in the centre that was belching smoke and which roared with such ferocity that the sound of the logs hissing and cracking echoed about the room. As they surveyed their new surroundings, they noticed a gathering of people towards the far wall. In the dim, flickering light, Falhinir and Sebastian could see Ecgferth and his most trusted knights seated beneath a large arched window. Falhinir could see the rain beating heavily against the glass, it was illuminated by wild streaks of forked lightning that tore through the dark skies, the threatened storm had clearly arrived. 'You may approach,' said Ecgferth, his sullen voice resounding throughout the vastness of the room. Beardy manhandled the pair further down the hall toward the seated men. Nervously, they approached the table occupied by the gathered knights.

As they got closer, Falhinir could see

that Ecgferth had hold of Asgrim's sword that had been taken from him when he was captured on the battlefield. It was the last that Falhinir expected to have seen of it. He was startled to see it again and watched intently as Ecgferth inspected the blade and the pommel with great curiosity. 'You, boy!' the King called out, looking at Falhinir, 'Where did you get this?' Falhinir detected a suspicious tone in his voice.

'It belonged to my uncle,' replied Falhinir, 'he was a knight of the Brotherhood of the Sword. Upon his death I became the custodian of the sword and a knight of the Order.'

'I see,' said the King. He had heard of the Brotherhood, but feigned a distinct lack of interest in knowing any more. 'So, your Order has made an alliance with Æthelred and now fights alongside his army?' he spat accusingly at the boy.

'We serve no army, we are simply poor pilgrims travelling through these lands!' Sebastian interjected., laying on thick the grovelling and fawning of a serf of the lower orders.

'Then what is your destination?' asked Ecgferth, slightly dubious as to the honesty of the pair having noted the charade that Sebastian was offering for his benefit.

'The mountains in the lands of the Celts,' replied Falhinir.

Ecgferth handed the sword to one of his knights, rose from his seat and went and stood beside the roaring fire, warming his rear on the heat from the flames. 'What is up there for you?' he asked, looking toward the sorry looking pair in front of him. Sebastian was still covered in mud from slipping down the bank and had a few bits of twig sprouting from his unkempt clothing. Falhinir still looked like the puny sixteen-year-old boy he was. Despite having honed his muscles in the time since he had left Romney Marsh, he still had not yet filled out the shape of a man.

Falhinir slowly approached the King, speaking directly to him and with his back to the table and the other knights assembled. He addressed his captor honestly. 'There is an evil, Sire, an evil that preys upon this land. His name is Tuan and he seeks to enslave these islands and all of its people. Only the great witch Ceridwen has the power and means to defeat him. The Brotherhood fought to destroy Tuan, but they were not strong enough and all but a few of their number were slain. This is our last chance to finally defeat him, while he is still weak. He is growing in strength and if we do not hurry, he will be unstoppable and we will all be lost.........' He tailed off and turned toward the other knights and Sebastian, his back to the King.

Ecgferth glanced up at Falhinir, the flickering glow of the fire giving the King a sinister appearance. 'There is much evil in this land and I am afraid that there is nothing you or anyone else can do about it.' He countered succinctly. The King's mind was clearly on more earthly matters and he was in no mood to listen to fanciful tales. Falhinir could sense that the moment was lost and Ecgferth's temper was beginning to rise. His face began to contort with a rage fuelled by frustration. 'I want to know the whereabouts of my brother! Tell me where he is!' He spat.

'Your brother?' replied Falhinir, 'We've got absolutely no idea where he is. We have not been travelling with Æthelred. We did not even know that your brother had been taken' he pleaded.

'He speaks the truth!' cried Sebastian hoping the king would realise that they were nothing to do with the kidnap.

The King pondered for a few moments. 'Then I am sorry,' he said softly, 'you are of no use to me.' The King turned away from Falhinir and returned to his seat. 'You will die on the morrow!' Ecgferth signalled to Beardy and his guards who seized the pair roughly now that they were of no further use to the king. Falhinir tried to struggle free, but the guards had them tightly in their grasp. They dragged him and Sebastian from the hall and away across the sodden courtyard back to the dungeons below.

Arnor and Æthelwulf glanced around

suspiciously. The deeper into the labyrinth they travelled, the more shadows and mysterious whispers of the caves had unnerved them. They had not come across anything tangible yet, but their minds had started to play tricks on them.

'We are almost there, about a quarter of a mile to go,' said Gwion, as they plodded deeper into the caves and further away from the sanctuary of the tomb. The path they were following was easy enough to walk but caves to the right and left could have led anywhere. It would have been virtually impossible to navigate without expert knowledge of the cave system. Suddenly an unearthly sound echoed through the chambers, filling the four with terror. It stopped them in their tracks and they stood in silence for a few seconds, reluctant to continue until the source of the sound became clear. They did not want to stumble onto something unawares.

'What the hell was that?' whispered Gwion nervously.

'I don't know,' replied Æthelwulf, 'but

I'm sure we will find out soon enough. Let's keep moving forward. The sooner we are out of here, the better. I think I'd prefer the rain and open sky to these sinister caves'

Silently, they crept through the caverns, the sound seemed to increase in volume with every step. A deep, terrible groaning sound, it echoed all about them, chilling them to the bone.

'Whatever it is, I think we are going toward it' said Morvan.

"I saw something!' exclaimed Gwion, pointing frantically into the darkness away to the left.

'Quiet!' ordered Æthelwulf in a loud whisper.

Cautiously, they continued down the path. Arnor and Æthelwulf drew their swords. The sound grew louder as they followed the path into a network of interconnected caves. There was only one way in and one way out. Æthelwulf told Gwion and Morvran to wait while he and Arnor went on ahead to investigate. The two guides, were only too happy to hang back and let the two more well-armed knights tackle whatever it was. It wasn't very long before the knights reached the source of the strange sound. Æthelwulf peered from behind the cave wall and what was before him made his blood run cold. Arnor stood behind his friend and peered over his shoulder.

The two men could not believe what they were seeing as they both held their breath in horror. In front of them, just a few feet away, striding through the stalagmites, was the most hideous creature they had ever laid eyes on. The thing was about six feet tall and thick set, Its shoulders were hunched over with leathery skin protruding through the torn material that hung from its back. Its arms were long and powerful, ending in claws that looked like they could tear a man in half. It was emitting an unhealthy greenish tinge which was all that it needed to navigate its way through the subterranean world.

'What the hell is that?' whispered Arnor.

Æthelwulf held up his hand, signalling

Arnor to be quiet. 'If that thing turns around, we will be in some serious trouble,' he warned.

The creature suddenly stopped mid-stride. Æthelwulf felt his heart miss a beat. Slowly, the beast turned its head from side-to-side sensing that there was someone or something close. Arnor held his arm up to his mouth, as his stomach wretched. For the beast that stood before him was utterly repulsive. The eyes had been ripped out and only scarred sockets remained where they should have been. The rest of the creature's face could only be described as shredded. The mandible was exposed, torn strands of mutilated flesh hung from the cheekbones, showing the creature's razor sharp and jagged teeth. Streams of blood tinted saliva, drooled from its open jaw. It sniffed at the air with the open slits that were all that was left of its nose, but could not get the scent of the two knights. It sniffed this way and that but the damage to its olfactory senses was too great. It grunted in disappointment at not knowing which way to go, then took off randomly in the opposite direction away from the two knights. It could sense they were there but had made the wrong call.

Arnor stepped out from behind Æthelwulf, breathing a sigh of relief as the beast wandered away into the darkness. 'What was that most hideous of creatures?' he asked.

'I have seen them once before, long ago,' said Æthelwulf, 'but never this far South. The last time I encountered them was upon the moors of Elmet. My people call them Mancus. Nobody knew where they came from, but they could lay waste to entire settlements, they make light work of devouring men. We must warn the others.'

'What was it?' asked Gwion as Arnor and Æthelwulf reappeared in the torchlight where Morvran and him were waiting.

'It was a terrible creature,' replied Arnor, still shocked from the encounter.

'The Mancus,' said Æthelwulf drily.

'I have heard of them,' replied Morvran, 'but I thought they were myth.'

'That was no myth we saw back there!' Arnor interjected.

'According to legend, they are the product of the sorcerer Landraar's evil deeds' explained Morvan 'Once men, they are now crippled and deformed creatures, forced to survive on the flesh of humans. The have been driven mad by an unimaginable hatred and disgust of their own existence. They were eventually banished from these lands and driven North, but no one could be certain of how many there were.'

'Well, it would appear that there is at least one still around,' said Arnor.

'Yes,' agreed Æthelwulf, 'we must tread carefully.'

Nervously, they continued into the foreboding darkness, their heightened senses reacting fearfully to the slightest sound or the merest shadow. The caves had widened out again with paths crisscrossing the one they were following. They had only journeyed for a short while longer when the flame of their torch began to flicker in a cool draught. They knew that the existence of fresh air in the caves must mean they were close to the entrance of the fort's dungeons.

'Hurry, we must go this way,' said Morvan and the others promptly followed.

'What was that?' Gwion asked, wiping something sticky from the back of his neck. The others turned and were horrified to see the Mancus looming over Gwion.

Arnor and Æthelwulf drew their swords but it was too late. Gwion tried to escape but the creature stretched out a hideously scarred and decayed arm. Grabbing him by the neck, the Mancus killed him instantly.

'Run!' shouted Arnor dashing away as fast as he could.

As they did so, the creature began to lumber after them, still holding the limp body of Gwion in its twisted and warty claw. It was surprisingly agile for such a deformed beast but it was no match for three grown men fleeing for their lives.

'Quickly! In here' called Morvan and the

other two followed. The trio found themselves in a small cave away from the main pathway and crouched in the darkness. Gwion had dropped the torch when the Mancus had set upon them and they were now relying on instinct and Morvan's knowledge of their surroundings. They could hear the fearful sound of the beast approaching from the depths of the cave beyond. Suddenly it stopped and there was silence. After a few moments where everyone held their breath, waiting, there came the horrible sound of bones cracking. Morvan peered out from the entrance to the cave. He could see the creature crouched down beside the torch. Not wanting to let its food get cold, the Mancus had decided to sit and enjoy its meal. Morvan could not contain himself and splattered the ground with vomit as he watched his friend being devoured. The Mancus bit into the top of Gwion's skull and prised open the top of his cranium. The despicable creature then proceeded to scoop the contents of poor Gwion's skull into its own mouth, as if it were eating porridge with its fingers.

While the Mancus was busy with its supper, the others saw their chance to flee. After witnessing what it had done to Gwion, they were more determined than ever to put as much distance between themselves and the beast as possible. Quickly, but as silently, they headed towards a dim light shining from the entrance to another cave.

'No! The other way! The other way!' exclaimed Sebastian as Falhinir attempted to work his shackles loose from the cave wall.

'I am turning it the other way!' Falhinir snapped in reply.

'Well, then turn it back the other way then!' came Sebastian's exasperated response, attempting to motion the direction with his head but looking more like he suffered from some sort of palsy.

'Will you *please* be quiet!' Said Falhinir sharply.

'I am only trying to help.' replied Sebastian sulkily.

'Yeah? Well, you're not, so shut it! Alright?' Falhinir barked at him, frustrated that they were right back where they had started, in the dungeon.

'Do you always bicker like this?' asked one of the other prisoners.

'Only when trying to get out of difficult situations!' said Falhinir, straining his voice as he pulled at the chains. 'Its no good, I can't get them to move at all. We are well and truly scuppered this time' he sighed, the sweat running from his brow.

'That's it then,' said Sebastian miserably, 'we die in a few hours.'

'That's as maybe, but you've still got a few a few hours to go,' came a familiar voice.

Falhinir recognised it immediately and was flooded with relief. 'Æthelwulf!' he exclaimed, 'How did you get in here?'

'There's no time to explain now,' Arnor interrupted, 'Where are the guards?'

'They went off in that direction,' said one of the other prisoners, nodding to the right.

Æthelwulf could see a guard

standing at the far end of the series of caves. Quietly, he crept up behind him, lifted his dagger from its sheath and plunged it through the unsuspecting man's throat, preventing him from making a sound. Hastily, he grabbed the keys dangling from the guard's belt before the limp body hit the ground.

'This place is heavily fortified,' said Falhinir as he was released from his chains. 'I don't know how you got in here, but it would be a good idea to go out the same way.'

'No, it wouldn't!' snapped Arnor whilst helping to release the other prisoners. 'I'd rather face a hundred soldiers than one of those things!'

'What we need is a diversion,' said Morvran.

'Falhinir,' said Æthelwulf, 'you can run faster than any of us here, I have an idea that will keep Ecgferth's soldiers busy for a while and give us a chance to escape the way we came in. We followed a path through the caverns that riddle this hillside and for over a mile away into the distance. But down in the caverns is a beast, a Mancus.'

'A what?' interrupted Falhinir.

'Just listen,' replied Æthelwulf, 'you will have to go down there and draw its attention, then run as fast as you can, back here, bringing the beast with you. Now, these things are big and they take huge strides, if one catches you, it *will* kill and eat you, so you will have to be quick.' Falhinir looked at Æthelwulf, wide-eyed with disbelief and fear, but before he had a chance to say anything Æthelwulf continued. 'I want you to shout when you are near the entrance to these caves. We will attract the attention of the soldiers and get them to come down here to see what the fuss is about. We will get them to follow us into the caverns below and right into the path of the Mancus. Once there we will hide in one of the side caves and let the Mancus take care of the soldiers for us. Once it realises there is food around it will prey upon the rest of the castle killing as many of the soldiers as it can. Whilst it is occupied with Ecgferth's men, we can make our escape.'

'That sounds like suicide!' yelled Arnor, rather alarmed at the prospect of seeing a Mancus up close again.

'It *is* dangerous but in the absence of a better plan, it will distract the soldiers long enough for us to escape,' said Æthelwulf. He turned and faced Falhinir. 'Will you do it Falhinir?' he asked.

'Where do I have to go?' he sighed, knowing full well that he had little choice but to go and seek the fearful beast in order to save the others.

The others looked on as Æthelwulf led Falhinir into the caverns to put their plan into action, explaining what the Mancus looked like and how best to attract its attention.

'What's a Mancus?' asked Sebastian nervously, knowing full well that he didn't really want to know the answer.

'A lethal beast that wants to eat us,' replied Morvan calmly, thinking about

Gwion and what had happened to him.

‘Oh,’ Sebastien sighed, ‘Still, it could be worse.’

Chapter VIII
Escape

Falhinir was feeling apprehensive as Æthelwulf led him to the entrance of the deep caverns.

'You will have to walk quite a long way into the caverns but make sure you stick to the main path or you'll get lost,' said Æthelwulf. He pointed to an opening in the rock. 'I will be waiting in this cave entrance here, when you get back. I'll pull you in when you run past.'

'Just as long as you do! He exclaimed

A thought occurred to Falhinir as he followed the knight 'Why do you think this beast has never left the caves before?' He asked looking at his friend nervously.

'I can't really say,' replied Æthelwulf, 'but it is definitely going to leave now! Good luck!' He said, turning to go back along the path.

Falhinir smiled at Æthelwulf as he too turned and walked away into the darkness, he could feel his heart pounding and his blood racing through his veins. His breathing was loud and heavy as he made his way further in. He didn't know what he was looking for, but he knew he would recognise it as soon as he laid eyes upon it. Slowly, he crept through the dark, mysterious caverns, a dim torch his only guide.

He had been walking for a short while when he caught sight of something in the shadows. It was a few feet away from him. He wiped the sweat from his brow with his sleeve and cautiously approached dark mass. As he got closer, he could make out that it was something terrible, it was once the body of a man. It was Gwion. Falhinir's stomach began to churn as he inspected the grim remains. Although the body had been gnawed and there were clearly bits missing, including a whole arm with teeth marks clearly visible on the shoulder, a look of sheer horror had been retained in the dead man's face. Falhinir stepped carefully over the dead man, making sure he did not tread on the small fragments of shattered skull and brain that was spattered on the ground all around the mutilated corpse.

He had only taken a few steps further when he heard a terrible groaning emanating from the darkness. *It could only be the Mancus,* Falhinir thought and knew then he had found what he was looking for. The sound chilled him to the core but not wanting to go any further into the depths of the caverns than was necessary, he stood silently, waving his torch from side to side. As he did so, he started to feel vibrations in the ground. He stood firm, not knowing what to expect would emerge from the caverns. His whole body tingled with anxiety as he detected a dark shape moving swiftly towards him. 'Here I am!' he shouted. 'Come and get me!'

Suddenly, the creature leapt from the shadows and began moving with remarkable agility for something so cumbersome, towards the terrified boy. As the Mancus became visible in the torchlight,

Falhinir was startled and disgusted by the creature's hideous appearance. Falhinir waited until the creature was close. He needed to make the creature follow him, he did not want to outrun the beast. If it had never left the confines of the caverns, all he needed to do was make sure that it could find the way to the surface. As he stood, waiting silently in the faint torchlight for the beast to approach, he was aware of his every sinew poised for escape. It was taking all his courage to stand in the creature's path and not just run for his life as fast as he could. Gradually he became aware that the vibrations beneath his feet had started to become more intense. As he looked about him, tearing his eyes away from the fearful creature advancing down the path towards him, he realised he was stood at a sort of crossroads in the caves. There were crisscrossed paths going off in all directions, each leading to a different cavern and another part of the cave system. It occurred to him that Æthelwulf had been right, it would be easy to get lost in these caves.

Each path looked pretty much the same. The thundering noise and vibrations all around him became ever stronger. It didn't take him long to realise that he was being approached by at least a dozen of those terrible things! He had been warned by Æthelwulf that there were likely to be more than just the one of those creatures down here. It stood to reason that where there was one, there was likely to be more. He hadn't expected there to be a pack of the damn things. The disturbance caused by the death of Gwion and the presence of the others in the caves must have drawn them from the lower depths.

'Bloody hell!' he yelled. Spinning on his heels, he began to run back down the path towards the surface as fast as he could. He followed the path to where it made a sharp turn to the left. He risked a quick glance over his shoulder to make sure he was keeping a safe distance between him and the pack or was it a herd of Mancus' that followed. What do you call a group of Mancus' he thought fleetingly as he returned his concentration to the path ahead of him. It was too late, suddenly he felt something solid against his right foot and he stumbled forward onto the hard ground. He put his hands out to break his fall and found himself at the same height as the crumpled remains of the partly consumed Gwion. He managed to scramble to his feet just as the beasts caught up with him. Leaving the torch on the ground, he began to run towards the light of the tunnel exit. As he ran, Falhinir could hear the awful sound of Gwion's body being crushed under his pursuer's feet.

Falhinir had nearly reached the entrance to the castle's dungeons when he realised that there was nothing behind him. He stopped and risked turning around to look behind him. Nothing. He could see nothing, hear nothing, feel nothing. Not being the most intelligent of creatures, Falhinir began to think that the beasts couldn't see where he'd gone or they had forgotten why they were chasing him in the first place but the truth was, they had found a much quicker exit from the caverns.

Falhinir stood panting heavily, his eyes twitching, searching the darkness. He leant against a wall, mopping his brow wondering whether to go back and try and lure the Mancus again. A prospect that did not appeal to him in the slightest, when he thought about it. Having realised that the Mancus' were their only hope of escape, he stood catching his breath. He was just readying himself to plunge back into the caves searching for the beasts, when fragments of shattered rock began raining down on him from above. The force of the rockfall left him no choice but to curl up on the ground covering his head. The Mancus' had broken through an entire cave wall and entered the dungeons of the fortress above by the most direct route. Falhinir began to desperately crawl away from the falling the debris, it was clear that the beasts had caused some sort of landslip in the caves and he was right underneath it. Suddenly Falhinir felt a sharp pull on his arm, it was Æthelwulf, who was waiting for him, just as they had planned. Æthelwulf dragged him into the dark depths of an adjacent cave well away from the falling rock outside.

Æthelwulf placed his hand over Falhinir's mouth to muffle his heavy breathing, just as another Mancus arrived at the entrance of the cave. The commotion must have drawn every single one of them to the surface. Their plan was in danger of being a little too successful. They would never be able to escape if there were too many more of them. They watched nervously as the creature took a sniff in the air, and began wiping the drool from its jaw. Fortunately, the beast was distracted by shouting and it lumbered away toward the light and the rest of the foul assembly.

'Guards! Guards!' yelled the voices. It was the free prisoners accompanied by Sebastian and Arnor. 'The prisoners are escaping!' they lied. It didn't take long for the guards above to come down to investigate. Before long, the sound of many feet descending the stone steps to the dungeon could be heard and it didn't take long for the Mancus to see them either. The soldiers were trapped in the narrow corridors with others coming up from behind. The creatures cut through them like it was an endless buffet line. It was hideous to behold and Arnor and the others ran into various caves to avoid being gathered into the melee. When a few of the guards managed to reach the bottom of the steps they were greeted by even more of the hungry beasts who were late to the party having had to travel from the furthest reaches of the cave system. It would appear that once their bloodlust was up, the Mancus' were insatiable. Having realised that something terrible was going on in the dungeons, the guards turned tail and fled back up the steps and into the fort, screaming as their companions were mutilated and devoured by the Mancus.

From their respective caves, the escapees could see the Mancus slowly climbing the staircase, intent on wreaking havoc on the rest of the fortress. The cries of Ecgferth's soldiers could be heard as the group began to emerge from their hiding places.

'Alright, where now?' asked Arnor. 'I say we go back out through the caverns.'

'We can't,' said Falhinir flatly.

'What, why the hell not?' asked Arnor angrily. 'Those things have all gone up the stairs into the fort, even if they haven't, there can't be many left down there surely!'

'My sword, I have to get my sword, I can't continue without it.' Falhinir replied urgently.

'There is always something!' shouted Arnor. 'Why is nothing straight forward!'

The others stared at the knight in amazement, for until now he had taken everything in his stride and approached situations logically and rationally. The last few hours in the caves had clearly shaken the seasoned trouper to the edge of his limits.

'I know where to get the sword,' said Falhinir, 'you all get out of here; I will meet you where the paths cross, just down and to the east of here.'

'We are not splitting up Falhinir,' said Æthelwulf, "we must remain together'.

Cautiously, they climbed the stairs, the cries of soldiers and the sound of the fort being torn apart becoming louder with every upward step. When they reached the top of the staircase, Falhinir carefully prised open the door that led into the courtyard. The soldiers had tried to barricade the door from the outside but it had not been a success. Everywhere he looked were half eaten bits of Ecgferth's soldiers. 'This way,' he told the others picking his way across the limb and torso strewn courtyard. Falhinir led them towards the main hall where he and Sebastian had met with Ecgferth earlier. The great door was swinging on its hinges but in order to get there they had to cross the courtyard. Several soldiers were fighting a Mancus who seemed to be enjoying playing with its food.

'There's no way to get past them!' exclaimed Sebastian, ducking to avoid the leg that the Mancus was waving about like some macabre club. The creature was blocking their way forward. They could see entrance to the great hall and beyond that the long table below the glass window. The fire pit had been left unattended and great flames were leaping toward the timbers holding up the roof. In order to get to the room and search for Falhinir's sword they would have to tackle the Mancus and the soldiers in front of the doorway.

The Mancus was clearly beginning to tire of the soldiers and with one final sweep of the grisly club, it sent the soldiers crashing into a wall, killing most them instantly and fatally wounding the others. The sound of crunching bone was almost more than they could bear and Falhinir distinctly saw Sebastian wince as the soldiers hit the wall. The Mancus swung round as Arnor gasped in horror and turned to Falhinir and the others who knew only too well there was nowhere for them to run, except past the creature.

'Run Falhinir!' cried Æthelwulf. 'We'll keep this thing busy!' He and the others began throwing anything they could find at the creature to divert its attention from Falhinir. This seemed to work for an instant, allowing Falhinir to run straight towards it and at the last-minute swerve around it towards the open door and the inner chambers of the fortress.

It was too much to hope the creature would be content with the slaughter it had already inflicted. Sure enough, it turned and focused all its attention on Falhinir who was weaving between its legs trying to get to the open doorway and the smoke billowing out from within. The others gave chase and followed the Mancus into the Great Hall. The creature had just caught up Falhinir as they entered. Arnor ran towards the Mancus and began stabbing at it with his sword. Æthelwulf soon followed suit, but was thrown across the room with a casual backhanded swing of the makeshift club. Arnor meanwhile, had managed to leap on the creature's back and was riding it like a grisly show pony. He raised his sword and thrust it deep into the Mancus' skull. The creature wavered in the air for a few moments before falling to the ground, with an almighty thud. It was dead.

'Thank you Arnor,' said Falhinir, breathing a sigh of relief, as Arnor picked himself up, having thrown clear.

As Sebastian was helping Æthelwulf to his feet he heard a voice. 'Help! Help!' it cried. The voice was coming from beneath a pile of masonry and timber where part of the hall roof had collapsed. By now smoke was engulfing the room as the roof timbers began burning with a fierce savagery. Falhinir and Arnor began scrabbling at the rubble. As they cleared the stone away, the body of a man began to emerge. It was Ecgferth, he had been buried when the Mancus burst into the hall, and the ceiling had collapsed. They pulled him free; he was battered and bruised, but alive. Not far from him, Falhinir could see the glint of a sword. He reached into the debris and picked it up. Æthelwulf marched over to Ecgferth and held his sword to his throat, ready to push down upon it, when Arnor stopped him.

'Not like this,' he said, 'he is still a King. To die in battle is honourable, but this is murder. We are better than that.'

'We could stop this war right now!' exclaimed Æthelwulf, gazing down upon the terrified King.

'Not like this we won't,' Arnor insisted, 'if it is discovered that Ecgferth was murdered, the war could be prolonged. I know the war is a lost cause, but this can only make it worse.'

Æthelwulf replaced his sword in his scabbard. 'Let's get out of here before the whole roof falls in,' he said turning in disgust from the cowering monarch and stalking away.

Together, they dashed through the chaos that had by now engulfed the entire fort, to the stables, where they found sufficient of the horses had been spared. Apparently Mancus were not as partial to horseflesh as human flesh. They mounted as fast as possible rode out toward the gates. As luck would have it, the gates of

Midgard had been left open by the soldiers when they abandoned the fort in panic.

The fires of the burning castle illuminated the dark skies behind Falhinir and his companions as they rode towards the entrance of the ancient burial mound where Arnor and Æthelwulf had left their own horses and supplies.

'What are we going to do now?' asked Arnor.

'What do you mean?' replied Falhinir.

'We have no map to guide us,' Arnor continued exasperated.

'No map? Where is my bag?' asked Falhinir, looking at his friends with concern.

'On my horse,' said Æthelwulf.

Falhinir strolled over to Æthelwulf's horse and opened the worn leather pouch that hung from his pack. From it he pulled a torn and tattered parchment, upon which the map was drawn. 'I placed it in here before we took to the battlefield,' he said nonchalantly as he tucked the map into his tunic.

Æthelwulf chuckled to himself, shaking

his head in relief. Arnor was less amused. He didn't say anything as he mounted his horse.

Falhinir and Sebastian each mounted a horse as Æthelwulf addressed the freed prisoners that had followed them from the fort. 'You men must return to Æthelred, the troubled times are not yet over. Serve your King proudly, fight for what you believe in and you will be triumphant!'

One of the freed men stepped forward. 'Thank you,' he said, 'We all thank you for saving our lives.'

'You are most welcome,' Arnor replied somewhat shakily, the escape from Midgard had troubled him far more than he was yet prepared to admit.

Æthelwulf turned to Morvan. 'Please, tell the King that we were successful in our mission, and now must continue our journey north. We will return when we can.'

'Yes, of course,' Morvan answered, and with that, he and the other soldiers watched in silence as Arnor, Falhinir, Sebastian and Æthelwulf rode off over the hills and far into the distance. When they were out of sight the freed captives, turned their backs on Midgard and set off in the other direction to search for Æthelred,

It was almost midday when Falhinir rose from a deep slumber. They had allowed themselves a short rest to recuperate from the excitement from the day before. He lay still for a few moments, his hands behind his head, staring at the still dull, heavy skies. He was more than a little bothered by Arnor's irrational behaviour in the cave. His unpredictable changes of mood were unnerving. If he were not a seasoned soldier, his temperament might have been easier to understand. They were on a dangerous mission and the ease with which Arnor had changed his mood might then have been due to the nature of their journey. But he was a knight of some standing and maturity and such misgivings should have been expunged from his thoughts by now. If he was honest, he would have expected a more solid show of courage from the older man and it had changed his estimation of his character in Falhinir 's eyes. He wanted to ask Arnor the reason for his strange actions, but did not want to risk a confrontation. He decided that when the opportunity arose, he would try and put his misgivings to Æthelwulf. It was not a conversation he was particularly looking forward to.

Æthelwulf was the next to stir. He sat up, running his hands through his long black hair. Sebastian was snoring heavily, as he so often did. Falhinir was once more struck by the little fellow's ability to sleep anywhere with such enthusiasm. Arnor, who was already awake, was huddled around the warmth of a small fire. They had dared not risk anything larger as they were still in the vicinity of Ecgferth's troops and they didn't want to attract the attention of any enterprising raiding party looking to find favour with the King. Æthelwulf and Falhinir joined him, for the air was brisk and the slight wind bitingly cold.

'Are we far from Leicester?' asked Falhinir, rubbing his hands together, attempting to bring some warmth to his body.

'About two hours North,' replied Arnor, 'from there it is an hour further on before we reach the edge of the Forest Lands.'

'Wake Sebastian,' said Æthelwulf, 'we have to ride fast if we are to reach the Forest Lands before nightfall. Also, we do not know how close those Warriors tread, we have left quite a spectacle in our wake and they will surely head towards such an unholy mess.'

After a hasty meal, the riders saddled up and headed North. They could hear the distant rumble of yet more thunder as they fast approached the city of Leicester. They drove their horses hard, for they did not want to be caught in yet another storm. As they approached the edge of the city, it was clear from some distance away, that it was heavily garrisoned.

Due to the nature of the wars in Middle Anglia, Leicester had been under no direct control. The townspeople had taken the decision to govern themselves and, with the exception of a few rural communities nearby, they contained the entire population within the hastily constructed city walls.

'I see no colours Æthelwulf,' stated Arnor looking towards the battlements and seeing nothing.

'What does that mean?' asked Falhinir curious as to why this should matter.

'It means...' interrupted Sebastian, 'It means that we have no way of knowing if we will be let in or killed! They could be enemies of Mercia *or* Deira, there is no way to know until it is too late to take cover.'

It was with great trepidation that the little band of travellers they approached the gates of the heavily fortified citadel.

Chapter IX
The
City of Leicester

'What is your business here?' bellowed a voice from the top of the huge stone wall.

'We are pilgrims, wishing to refresh ourselves before our journey takes us through the Forest Lands!' Arnor yelled in reply. The four of them stood before the great gates feeling slightly uncomfortable as many pairs of eyes and not a few weapons were trained on them from above. The horses fidgeted nervously as their riders waited to see whether they would be granted entry.

After what seemed like rather longer than was necessary, the sound of movement and shouted instructions could be heard from behind the huge oak doors. With much heaving and sounds of heavy objects being moved, they gradually began to creak open. As the four companions spurred their mounts cautiously through the gates, they were greeted by two heavily armed guards. They were both wheezing slightly as if they had had to move rather more swiftly than they were used to.

'You may enter,' said a tall, burly man clad in an assortment of old and slightly rusty armour, 'but you must leave all your weapons here at the gatehouse. There has been much trouble in recent times. We are taking no chances with strangers. Your weapons will be returned to you when you leave.' He sighed heavily after delivering his little speech. From his demeanour, Sebastian deduced that they had been the cause of the delay. It had taken them a while to don their armour and present a show of might to the unknown travellers below. A smile played around his mouth but he chose to say nothing. There was no point in antagonising the two lazy guards any more than necessary.

'Very well,' Arnor replied, he looked around at the others who were uncertainly clutching their weapons a little more tightly. The old knight reluctantly handed over his sword, he was also not happy about the arrangement, but knew they had no choice if they were to allay the suspicions of the townsfolk. The others followed suit without any enthusiasm. When they had finished, a rather unhealthy-looking pile of weapons, especially for a bunch of pilgrims to be carrying, was piled by the gatehouse. The guards had raised their eyebrows a little at some of the places Sebastian had produced daggers from but they too chose not to address the strange little man who seemed to have a weapon concealed in every fold of his clothing. Even Falhinir looked a little surprised but he had known Sebastian long enough now not to question him about such matters. He took the chance to look around rather than catch Sebastian's eye, trying to get his bearings within the confines of the city walls.

Inside their haven, a thriving community was bustling about its business. There was a market in full swing in the square directly in front of them. The air was filled with the smell of the various local produce being touted by the local farmers. There was also a wide variety of live animals and birds squawking, quacking, squeaking and generally making racket. There were merchants, townsfolk and the usual rag covered bundles of beggars all yelling and shouting their wares and trying to attract your attention. It was a typical market, for a large settlement but Falhinir had only been used to the village market held every other Saturday in Romney. This was a much more raucous affair and he was awestruck by the variety and colour of the various things that were being bought and sold. Not to mention the fat glistening carcasses of beasts already slaughtered and ready for the table. Sebastian was staring at the fresh salmon piled up and glassily staring at the passing customers from a cold slab. He had not eaten anything other than bread and cheese for almost two days, which in his opinion was not nearly sufficient sustenance for a constitution such as his. The sound his stomach was making sounded like whale song and that could not be good in anyone's book. He thought.

'We will eat soon enough,' said Arnor, dragging the hungry little fellow away from the stall. 'I think it would be best if Æthelwulf and I tend to the supplies, while Sebastian and the boy arrange food and drink,' he continued. Falhinir eagerly pointed to the nearest but rather unsavoury looking alehouse, 'We will meet you in that inn.' He strode purposefully toward the entrance before anyone could stop him. Sebastian sighed and thinking to himself "I'm getting too old for all this' he trudged after the lad, knowing full well there would be no fresh salmon on the menu where they were going.

Æthelwulf and Arnor soon disappeared, blending easily into the milling crowds of the market. Falhinir and Sebastian crossed the low beamed entrance of the rather tatty looking inn and were surprised to find the main taproom was almost as busy as the market place. The alehouse was alive with people from all over the country. It was rather cosy, in fact a lot more pleasant inside that it had looked from the exterior. Falhinir pushed his way to the counter and ordered a large flagon of ale. He had already downed one large cupful and had poured himself another before Sebastian had managed to reach his side through the melee. A hearty fire roared in the hearth and beside it sat a storyteller. He had gathered quite a crowd about him who were hanging on his every word. He had just reached the end of a particularly grizzly story and the crowd responded with the customary groans and applause. He was keen not to lose too many of his audience before he could persuade a few coins or at least something to drink from them so he launched immediately into another tale before they could drift away. Falhinir poured Sebastian a cup of ale, taking the opportunity to finish his own and pour himself another generous measure.

'Steady on, lad' Sebastian counselled, 'you know what happened last time'.

"Don't be such an old spoilsport' Falhinir scoffed 'I know what I'm doing. That was mead I was drinking before, this is ale, I know exactly what I'm doing with ale.......' he was nodding vigorously as he said this making himself look rather simple again. Still keeping his own counsel, Sebastian just sighed and turned his attention to the storyteller. The well-practiced artist had his audience captive again as he told a new tale of an evil sorcerer who had succeeded in creating monsters by mating women with huge beasts. He had lost control of the resultant unnatural horrors and they had eventually escaped. The hideous monsters caused immense damage and spread fear to the surrounding countryside around the city.

'They had developed a taste for human flesh.' he said, causing horrified gasps from the audience. Some of the crowd looked around fearfully at their fellow drinkers, so caught up in the narrative were they. The storyteller went on to tell how they had been beaten back to secret caves hidden beneath an ancient Roman fortress somewhere around these parts. Falhinir had been listening with rapt attention to every word the minstrel said and was poised to give the exact location of the caves a few miles south of the city and what they had encountered there when Sebastien put his hand firmly over the young man's mouth to shut him up. Sebastian dragged him away from the minstrel before he could say another word and land them in any more trouble.

"Here, drink this" he muttered shoving another flagon of ale roughly into the boy's chest. Falhinir looked at it puzzled and began to drink deeply from it. Sebastian figured that it was time for them to leave the warmly lit taproom and try and find a quiet corner to sit and wait for the others. They walked through the inn into a smaller, more dimly lit room. It was occupied by a small group of six hard-faced men playing dice in the far corner and using the light from a single candle to illuminate their game. The wary pair approached the bar keeper, made their order for more ale and something to eat and sat down as far away from the suspicious looking group as they could. Neither of the companions spoke as they sipped their ale and eyed the dice players warily.

'You lying cheating bastard!' came a loud yell from one of the men playing dice. Sebastian was in the process of taking yet another swig from his cup when he found himself being thrown forward as one of the large men leapt from the table and barged into the supping Falhinir. Wiping his ale from his startled face and looking round, he could see that the dice game had turned ugly. All six men were standing up eyeing each other menacingly. It was not possible to see which one of them threw the first punch but soon fists were flying all ways. The brawl between the six dice players soon attracted men from other rooms who, seeing a large fight in progress felt compelled to join in, even if they had no idea who was fighting who or what it was all about.

'It's the same the world over' yelled, Sebastian over the crowd, "Whenever a fight breaks out, a certain type of men think it is their moral duty to wade in' Falhinir and Sebastian had remained seated, attempting to distance themselves from the chaos around them but as men and furniture alike were thrown about the room, Falhinir felt that he too should be hitting someone. He stood and dragged off one of the dice players who had been flung across their tabletop. The weasel of a man, who was now semi-conscious, slid down the wall where he fell, his eye puffy and steadily oozing blood. He had been flung there by the fellow that had accused him of cheating and who had knocked Falhinir's beer over. Falhinir was just about to take up the subject of his spilled beer with the angry looking villain, who was looking around for someone to punch next, when he was hit over the back of the head with part of a chair. Pugilism had not been Falhinir's strongest area of combat, but the fact he was feeling particularly brave for some reason, was sufficient to encourage him to get some practice in. No doubt fired up by the huge quantity of ale he had consumed, he hurled himself into the crowd, throwing feeble and inaccurate punches at any target they could find. It wasn't long before he found himself in the thick of the fighting. There were several of the dice players who seemed to take issue with the young man joining in with 'their' fight and turned their attention on Falhinir himself. Several minutes and at least twice as many punches later, the brawl was broken up by three large fellows that had been drinking next door. By this time Falhinir was sitting on the floor, leaning up against the wall, wishing that he hadn't decided to get involved at all

'You bloody fool,' Sebastian chuckled to himself, looking at his young friend who was looking a bit battered, to say the least.

His attention was taken away from the boy to the food being laid on the table by a young kitchen hand. There was a whole salmon swimming in a sauce of parsley, with huge chunks of bread and a thick broth to accompany it.

“This is the speciality of the house’ the kitchen boy announced, ‘You can’t come to the Salmon Inn, without having it’ he continued with a flourish.

Sebastian’s eyes nearly popped out of his head, who would have thought that the idiot boy would have brought them to the best place in town. No wonder it was so busy he thought as he fell upon the veritable feast in front of him.

‘What’s wrong with him?’ Arnor asked Sebastian, pointing to Falhinir as he and Æthelwulf strode into the room sometime later.

‘Just a bit of harmless fun,’ Falhinir called out, stuffing more of the salmon and bread into his puffy face. He stood away from the table to allow the others to sit down, wiping the blood from his nose.

‘Harmless?’ remarked Æthelwulf, turning Falhinir’s head to one side to get a better look at his bruised eye and cheek. ‘Looks to me like you got a bloody good hiding!’ He and Arnor grinned at each other as they began to eat. They both knew what it was like when they had been Falhinir's age. Sebastian, who had already forgiven the boy, shoved more of the excellent salmon into his mouth, marvelling at how Falhinir had an uncanny ability to sniff out excellent hostelries. They spent a companionable afternoon in their own company in the back room of the inn. More candles had been lit and the dice players had been thrown out. Falhinir, who had already consumed more than sufficient ale, dozed happily in the corner as the others continued talking and drinking until it was time to go to sleep. They tried to wake the dozing Falhinir but the young man was having none of it. Eventually, Arnor and Æthelwulf hefted him upstairs one under each arm and slung him on the pallet in the corner of the room he was to share with Sebastian. Fortunately, the little old man had no problem dropping off and the four companions had a peaceful night beneath the rafters of the Salmon Inn.

The following morning, Falhinir awoke with an almighty headache, whether it was from the angry lump on his cranium where a fist had connected with it, or whether it was from the dehydration caused by ale, he couldn't say. Suffice to say their breakfast was a quiet and somewhat queasy affair as far as he was concerned. He had the distinct impression that the older three companions were laughing at him. Nothing was actually said but every time he sighed and tried to take another mouthful of food, they looked at each other and smiled. If he was honest, he would be glad to get out of the inn and into the fresh air. The sight of food was turning his stomach and he could only manage small sips of liquid at a time.

After they had eaten, they left the inn and began making their way towards the stables, where the provisions ordered by Arnor were due to be delivered. The four companions trudged along in silence as the narrow city streets made it difficult for them to walk more than two abreast. As Falhinir walked on, hoping to get to the stables first where he could have a rest before the others got there, he couldn't help but notice a hooded stranger coming towards him. The cloak that covered the stranger was of a finely spun cloth and the whole demeanour and character of the hooded figure seemed out of place in the narrow streets. As they passed each other in the narrow street, the mysterious figure raised their head and looked straight at him. Falhinir stopped walking. He was dumbfounded to be staring into the eyes of the most captivating woman he had ever seen. Her eyes were the darkest blue so much so that they were almost violet. He was held spellbound by her breath-taking beauty, her complexion was completely unblemished and fair, she had lips of the deepest red and the combination of her scent of meadow flowers and her utter loveliness was enough to completely stop him in his tracks. Barely able to breathe, he stood motionless for what seemed like an age. The woman turned her head away for a second, then looked up again at Falhinir.

Falhinir stepped back in horror as he found himself no longer staring in the face of beauty, but at the horrendous features of a hellish manifestation; there was no fair skin, no red lips and no eyes of blue, her skin was decaying, exposing most of the woman's skeletal features. Her razor-sharp teeth were pointed and covered in what looked like fresh blood and her blue eyes had been replaced with piercing red ones that would have looked more like cats' eyes had they not been blazing with utter hatred. The whole transformation struck terror into Falhinir's heart. He gasped and closed his eyes for a second. Within the blink of an eye, she had returned to her original beautiful state again. Falhinir looked away for a brief moment, trying to process what he had seen but when he looked up again, the woman was nowhere in sight. He looked up and down the long narrow street, but she had disappeared in that blink of his eye. He pondered for a second. *Could I have imagined it?* He thought to himself. *If I did, could there have been something wrong with one of those flagons of ale I drank yesterday? Causing me to hallucinate? No, I'm clearly not that ill, I definitely saw her and if that's the case then what did it mean?* The woman seemed real enough, and although the evil appearance only showed itself for an instant, he was absolutely certain of what he had seen. He decided not to tell his friends just in case they made fun of him again. They would definitely assume drink as a factor and he wouldn't get any sense from them at all. He began to walk again and realised that somehow the other three had gotten in front of him. That was odd, he thought, he had definitely been in front of them when the woman came up to him, yet now he was behind. It was something else that made the whole encounter somewhat unsettling but he thought it best to put the whole affair right out of his mind as he ran to catch up with the others.

'What happened to you?' asked Sebastian as Falhinir joined him at his side.

'I just got caught up for a moment,' he replied, looking back down the street.

'Well, we'd better get a move on,' said

Arnor, 'we need to make the Forest Lands before nightfall.'

It took them a little over another five minutes to reach the stables, Falhinir kept searching down every crossroads or lane they came across for the mysterious woman but he didn't catch sight of her once. Their horses were already saddled and waiting for them, their supplies stowed in various packs and saddlebags by the yard boys who were always obliging for a few extra coppers from travellers keen to be on their way. Once they had mounted, paid for the stabling and reacquainted themselves with their steeds, they headed back towards the gatehouse to collect their weapons. Sebastian's assumption about the gate guards had been correct, they found both men still asleep in the guardhouse, their pile of weapons pretty much where they had left them. The only exception were the two swords belonging to Arnor and Falhinir that had been taken from the pile and were laying across the solid table in the guardhouse. The remains of last night's meal was still in front of them and the guards were asleep with their elbows over the two swords. Arnor slid both swords carefully from under the noses of the sleeping guards, not making a sound and taking care not to disturb their elbows. He sheathed his own and handed the other sword back to Falhinir. Sebastian, meanwhile had set about concealing the vast array of weapons he carried in various places on his short stout body. It was a wonder that such a small man could conceal quite so much steel about his person. Seeing no reason to wake the guards from their slumbers and trouble them further, they slipped out of the city gates behind a large hay wagon that had already been given permission to leave. As they left the city, Falhinir cast hopefully over his shoulder, just in case the mystery woman had decided to follow them. He continued to look on as the huge wooden gates were closed behind him and his friends, once more shutting them out.

'What is it?' asked Sebastian. 'You have

been behaving very strangely since we left the inn, are you feeling alright?'

'I'm fine, it's nothing,' replied Falhinir.

'I think they may have hit you harder than you realised!' joked Sebastian, knowing full well that the effects of the ale were also being felt by the youngster. He turned his horse away from Falhinir and with Arnor and Æthelwulf they set off on the open track towards the forests and the final destination shown on their map.

There was little sun that day but when it did reveal itself from behind the clouds they saw it rise higher in the sky and then began to wane again as the four riders ate the miles towards the forestlands. This was open countryside and each of them felt exposed on the flat plains. It reminded Falhinir of the flat of the Romney marsh, meaning that their silhouettes were clearly visible for miles around and meaning too that there was scant cover to hide in should they be spotted. The knowledge that even though the Warriors had not been seen for some time, they were still out there, caused them all to be anxious. They all felt the collective need to reach the safety of the trees clearly visible on the horizon, but taking some time to reach. As the warmth of the day began to recede Sebastian pulled his cloak tightly around his fat little body, He was always the first to feel the cold, but it wasn't long before the others did the same. The season was beginning to turn, they were almost upon the end of autumn, and winter was just around the corner. They all knew it and were all silently hoping that their journey would not extend too long into the harsh climate. They were also aware that they had to get to the sanctuary of the trees before dark for this was not the time of year to be out in the open for too long. As they proceeded on their way across the open countryside, with the exception of a few hamlets scattered here and there, there had been nothing to relieve the landscape for miles around, no settlements, nothing.

'There!' shouted Æthelwulf, pointing. They had been racing towards a sort of escarpment, the trees they could see in the distance were some way into, rather than the beginning of the forest. No wonder they didn't seem to be getting any closer. The others looked on as they observed the beginning of the Forest Lands. There was nothing but dense woodland for as far as the eye could see. It was the largest collection of trees any one of them had ever encountered. The fact that they were searching for one individual in the vastness of this forest without any clear instructions on which way to go was not lost on any of them. They stopped so Falhinir could extract the precious map from inside his tunic.

'The map indicates there is an entrance to the forest by road just Northeast of here,' he said, pointing in the general direction. 'It is the only entrance shown as a way into the forest, I think we must go that way' he added, knowing full well that the map would be of no more use once they had entered the dense dark trees.

It was getting to the end of the

daylight as rode Northeast down the gentle escarpment toward the only entrance to the forest shown on their map.

'This is as far as the map will take us,' Falhinir told the others, 'all we can do is enter the forest and see what awaits us.'

Sebastian shuddered and looked all around as they slowly breached the threshold of the forest, passing from the remaining light of day into the darkness of the wood.

Chapter X
The
Forest Lands

The cold night air made the forest damp and uncomfortable as the four companions set up their shelter for the night. There was an uncanny claustrophobic feeling not being able to see the sky under the trees. Sebastian didn't enjoy not being able to see the stars at night but resigned himself to the thought that he might as well get used to it. They were on their own now with no help from the map. Their instructions so far had been clear. They now had no instructions; they could be in the forest months before they found Ceridwen. He sighed and shuffled around on the forest floor trying to arrange the leaves into a sort of nest where he could be comfortable for the night. Falhinir meanwhile was feeling confused. As he settled down for the night, he lay looking up at the canopy of rustling branches above him. He was trying to make sense of what he had seen in Leicester, but try as he might, he couldn't get the woman out of his mind. He was no nearer understanding what had happened as slowly he drifted into a deep dreamless sleep.

Only the creatures of the forest stirred as Falhinir awoke with a start later that night. Looking up at the night sky through the branches he could see that the clouds had moved on, revealing a full moon, that twinkled in the rustling of the trees. It was much warmer in the air and a thick fog had arisen under the trees at about waist height. It was a phenomenon that Falhinir knew well. It happened on the Romney Marshes all the time, the difference in temperature between the damp ground and the surrounding air caused a low fog to hang around the fields at home all the time, especially at night and early morning. It was an eerie sight to see the bases of the trees shrouded in a mysterious blanket of white but Falhinir was unafraid. He sat upright; not sure why he had woken. Suddenly he became aware that something was moving between the trees, causing the mist to swirl and shudder as the intruder skulked through the woodland. He looked around to the others but they were all still sleeping soundly. For some reason, he couldn't have explained why, he did not feel the visitor was hostile. It was certainly not a Warrior, they had a sort of 'presence' that accompanied them, since that day in Romney when Asgrim had been murdered, he had been able to feel when they were near him but had only recently begun to relax from the feeling of agitation that had followed them from London. This was something completely different and he felt strangely compelled to go and find out what it was. He rose from his blankets and decided to investigate. He ventured further into the dark depths of the forest disturbing the mist as he went. As he wandered amongst the tall oaks, the broken moonlight pervading the treetops, he seemed to awaken the forest from its nocturnal slumber; the shadows were ever changing, altering with the swirling mist and fog: the ground seemed to be crying out to him with every step. He was compelled by a force he could not recognise to follow the apparition further away from his companions and the safety of their meagre fire.

Slowly, as he followed the mysterious shape, he began to realise it was definitely a person. The shadows coalesced around the figure as they walked through the forest. Falhinir began to catch up but he was reluctant to make his presence known until he was sure the person was not threat to them. He was only a few feet away when the hooded stranger stopped and turned around to face him. Falhinir was both surprised and shocked to discover that the hooded stranger he had been following, was the woman from the alleyway he had seen in Leicester! The woman stood for a few moments as he revelled in her beauty, before gently swaying towards him. Falhinir could feel his pulse begin to race the closer she got to him.

Falhinir was captivated and stood, silently rooted to the spot facing the mysterious woman. He gazed bewilderingly at the stranger revelling in her gorgeousness; her pale complexion accentuated by the moonlight. She slowly raised her arm and held out her hand. He was so enthralled; all other thought left his mind except for the woman in front of him.

'Who are you?' Whispered Falhinir. Not wanting to startle her. She did not answer, and was silent as Falhinir raised his hand and put it in in hers. Her skin was soft, but cold and a little clammy. He stumbled slightly as she pulled him closer to her, she had surprising strength for such a delicate body. He was thrown a little off balance as she clasped him tightly to her. He could feel her breasts pushing into his chest as she held him against her. He stared intently into her eyes trying not to break the moment but anxious to see what was hidden there. She lifted her hand again and gently brushed it against Falhinir's face, her icy touch bringing a chill to Falhinir's sensitive skin. He began to feel the stirrings of arousal, and realised that the feelings he had felt in that region before had never been as intense as this. Maybe this was to be the time, maybe he was actually about to lose his virginity with this beautiful stranger. He closed his eyes in excited anticipation, he could feel her breath on his cheek as she moved her rosy red lips towards his own outstretched mouth...............

And Nothing............... before he could open his eyes, he suddenly felt himself being violently pushed backwards without warning. He fell to the ground banging his head hard as he fell, he heard a piercing scream and then silence. He could taste blood in his mouth as he opened his eyes, only to discover Æthelwulf standing over him with his sword held in his hand. The decapitated corpse of the woman was lying at his feet.

'My God!' Falhinir exclaimed. 'What have you done?'

'I have saved your life!' replied

Æthelwulf gruffly.

'What the hell from!' Falhinir shouted in reply.

'That was no woman, it was one of Morrigan's demons,' the knight said disgustedly, 'Tuan's power is growing, he now has the ability to summon the *Tuatha Dé Morrigan*, the people of the goddess Morrigan and that was one of them'.

'I saw her in Leicester, I didn't like to say anything, but it was when we were in the street, on our way to the stables. I thought I saw her fair features briefly turn to that of a hellish creature, but I thought it was my imagination,' Falhinir confessed to Æthelwulf somewhat sheepishly, his ardour deflating before their eyes.

'It was not your imagination,' said Æthelwulf, he carefully lifted the woman's decapitated head from the ground by her hair, turning the head towards Falhinir. Falhinir was revolted by the creature's true appearance and shuddered at the thought he had been just about to kiss it. He drew a veil in his mind as to what he had also been considering allowing the demon to do to him.

'They use their beauty to get close to their prey' Æthelwulf continued 'Tuan wants to know how close you are to Ceridwen, I'm sure of it.'

'How do you know of these demons and how could you be so sure that she was one of them?' asked Falhinir, getting up off the ground and wiping a few spatters of blood from his face with the back of his sleeve.

Æthelwulf placed his hand upon Falhinir's shoulder. In a fatherly fashion. 'By now you must realise that there is more to this world than that which you see around you. I have travelled these lands for most of my life, and seen wondrous marvels and terrors that no man should ever endure. You will too. Never accept everything for what it seems.'

There was something about Æthelwulf's words that drew Falhinir to the conclusion that there was more to this young knight than he had believed in the beginning. He did not know what made the man so special, but his knowledge of magic and witchcraft was extensive and he certainly knew how to take charge of a situation if the need arose. He looked on the knight with a renewed respect.

'Æthelwulf, why do you think Tuan wants to know how close we are to Ceridwen? I mean, why doesn't he just kill us?' Falhinir wondered.

'If we knew that Falhinir, we could solve this puzzle, it would also explain why we have not encountered any Warriors for some time. You must be on your guard from now on, not all demons will be so recognisable.' Æthelwulf knelt down and turned over the demon's wrist, revealing a peculiar scar. 'This is the mark of the Tuatha. I saw it when she raised her hand to your face. They can appear in many different forms, you must from now on take extra care when talking to strangers. Come. There will be no more tonight, we need to get some rest.'

As they started to return through the forest to their shelter, they were accompanied by the sound of heavy footsteps. It sounded like someone was running through the woodland. Cautiously, they drew their swords and waited.

'Is everything alright?' cried out a familiar voice. It was Arnor. He too had woken in the night and finding both Falhinir and Æthelwulf to be missing, had resolved to go in search of them.

'Yes, everything is fine,' Falhinir replied with more steadiness in his voice that he would have expected.

Arnor could see the headless corpse lying on the ground behind them. 'What is that?' he asked, curiously as he trod over a fallen branch to inspect the mysterious body.

'Tuan now has command of Morrigan's demons,' said Æthelwulf, his concern at having discovered this clearly audible in his voice.

Arnor walked to the body and turned the severed head over with his foot, the demon's hideous true appearance was once again revealed and he grimaced as he looked at it. 'We should be able to see these things coming from some distance!' he said jokingly, trying to conceal his revulsion at the sight of the creature.

'They are capable of altering their appearance as poor Falhinir has just discovered. They are a most dangerous enemy,' Æthelwulf said sternly turning away and leading the young man away from the scene.

Arnor stood for a moment, staring at the severed head it seemed to hold him in some sort of a trance

'Arnor!' Called Æthelwulf breaking the spell 'we must get some rest; we do not know what we face in the morning.' They trudged back to the camp to check on Sebastian. When they returned, they found that he had slept through the whole episode and was snoring heavily. Not even the creeping sounds of the wood could disturb him.

A dull, brooding sky had gathered over the forest during last few hours that the four had been sleeping. It was a few spots of early morning rain dripping from the trees overhead that awoke them.

'Which way should we ride?' Sebastian asked Falhinir grumpily even though he knew that the boy had no more idea than he had. 'We do not know who we are looking for, or where to find them, we could be riding these forests forever. I know that Vortigern said that whoever we are looking for will find us, but how do we know that we are in the part of the forest where he may be expecting us?'

Falhinir took out the map and unravelled it somehow hoping that now they were actually in the forest, a path would be revealed or another part of the map had somehow become visible. 'The map shows the entrance into the forest to be here,' he said, 'then nothing but trees.' Falhinir rolled up the map and placed it back in his bag. Standing up, he began to survey the woodland around him as if it might reveal a clue. As his eyes became accustomed to the gloom, he noticed that some of the trees were different to the others. A mysterious dew was coating the trunks and falling from some of the trees. As the strange moisture touched the ground, it began to emit a peculiar white glow. The longer he stared at it the more visible the way forward became. Falhinir became excited 'There is a visible path through the woodland,' Falhinir told his friends, pointing into the depth of the thick forest, 'This trail must lead us somewhere.' He began gathering his things and stuffing them in his saddlebags anxious to follow what little lead they had before it disappeared

'Well, it's better than nothing,' said Arnor, mounting his horse and preparing to follow where Falhinir led although he couldn't see any difference in the trees whatsoever.

The others did the same, and before long Falhinir was leading his friends along the tenuous path that took them deep into the dark forest, even though he seemed to be the only one of the four of them who could see the trail they were following. Sebastian had screwed up his eyes and allowed them to go out of focus hoping to see the path they were following but all it had done was make him cross eyed and caused him to become dizzy and in danger of falling off his horse. This was an indignity he wasn't prepared to contemplate so he merely followed meekly where the young lad led them.

After several hours of steady plodding, they came upon a large clearing. In the centre of the ground stood a huge oak tree, like a giant among the other trees. It was as though the other trees did not dare approach the giant specimen or encroach on the light and ground it occupied. Had they but known it, they had reached the centre of the Forest Lands.

Falhinir leapt down from his horse and walked confidently towards the tree. Upon further inspection he found the trunk to be almost completely hollow. Cautiously, he stuck his head inside.

'You must be Falhinir!' Intoned a voice from the darkness, startling the youngster. 'Come in, come in, and bring your friends with you!'

'Who are you?' Falhinir shouted into the darkness, 'show yourself!' As he peered down into the trunk of the might oak, he spotted a dim light rising from below him, gradually getting brighter as it neared the surface. A tall man carrying a torch soon hove into view walking up from a staircase made of tree roots that ascended from below the forest floor. Dressed in simple robes of brown, the man stood over six feet tall with a long white beard and dark brown eyes.

'Hello young man,' he said gently, 'I am very pleased to meet you at last. My name is Laravine.'

'Are you the one we seek?' Falhinir asked slightly confused. He had been expecting Ceridwen, a woman, not the tall monk like character in front of them.

'Seek? Found, I'd say!' he replied, followed by a raucous laugh, 'follow me!'

Falhinir waved at the others who had hung back from the tree, signalling them to follow him. They looked at each briefly before gingerly approaching the huge oak and following the strange pair into the centre of the hollow trunk and the staircase it contained.

'Vortigern said you would find us,' said Falhinir, following Laravine down the dark staircase, 'it was only by sheer luck that we found you.'

Laravine turned and faced Falhinir. 'Luck? Do you think I lay down that path for every traveller who enters these forests?'

Falhinir gave a slight chuckle and shook his head. 'No, I suppose not,' he replied. There was something kind and gentle about this old hermit that you couldn't help but warm to thought Falhinir, he was certainly friendly enough and the gullible youngster allowed himself to be led down the path under the mighty forest guardian.

One after the other Æthelwulf, Sebastian and Arnor shuffled into the trunk, and proceeded down the twisting stairs that would lead them into Laravine's home deep beneath the mighty oak tree. The four companions looked about them with a sense of unease. The huge chamber was adorned with ancient and mystic runes, carved into the huge roots of the oak that formed the walls and ceiling of the enormous room below. Extending from the corners of the room like buttresses, ancient and fearsome figures were intricately carved into the wood.

Laravine walked over to a large pot hanging over a small, carefully contained fire. A delicious smell of warm broth permeated the air. He had clearly prepared it in anticipation of his guest's arrival and the smell of it caused Sebastian's whale song to call out again and reverberate round the tunnel before he had even entered the room.

'Sit, sit! You must be hungry, you cannot have eaten yet,' he said ignoring the belly rumblings of the little man as he poured a generous measure of the thick soup into five wooden bowls.

Arnor and Æthelwulf were the next to enter followed by Sebastian who had been the last to enter the staircase. As they assembled in the large room, Laravine broke into a huge smile. 'Sebastian! How are you? It is wonderful to see you again!'

'Old friend,' Sebastian exclaimed in reply, 'I had no idea! How marvellous it is to gaze upon you once more!'

The others had never seen Sebastian so animated, not even when being chased by Dark Warriors! He and Laravine had first met over forty years earlier whilst they were both serving King Oswald of Northumbria, but had not seen each other for many years.

'What are you doing here?' Sebastian asked, looking up at his tall friend. 'There have been many times over the years when I would have welcomed your council.'

Laravine looked at Sebastian softly. 'I know what happened at Dumnonia, I am sorry. I am also sorry that you must face Tuan once more, all of you.' He looked straight at Falhinir. 'There is nothing that can prepare you for what lies ahead. There are difficult times coming, you must be strong, if the prophecy is to be fulfilled. You must succeed and to do so you must learn all there is to know about each other. There can be no secrets. Please,' Laravine gestured at the table, 'please come and sit, for now we eat.'

Falhinir and his friends sat at a large table as Laravine handed them each a bowl of the broth. As Laravine went to sit down he was overcome by an uneasy feeling that caused him to frown. He did not know what it meant, but its presence was strong.

'Is everything alright?' asked Sebastian, noticing his friend was looking somewhat pale.

'Yes, fine,' Laravine replied, glancing at his guests with a smile, 'I am sorry for being distracted.' Looking at Arnor and Æthelwulf, he said, 'I am pleased to welcome you into my home, Arnor of Merion and Æthelwulf of Warwick.'

Arnor and Æthelwulf looked at each other. 'How do you know our names?' asked Arnor.

'Laravine is a powerful Druid,' said Æthelwulf, not allowing Laravine a chance to answer, 'your name has been spoken to me on more than one occasion.' Laravine gave Æthelwulf a friendly smile. 'Alas, I am not as powerful as once I was. Old I have become, but I can still see much of what is around me.'

They were happily munching their way through the excellent soup and fresh bread that had appeared on the table when Laravine interrupted the silence once more. 'Why has May not told your King the truth, Æthelwulf?'

Æthelwulf looked up at the old hermit surprised by his words. 'The truth?' he asked.

'Yes,' Laravine replied, 'Æthelred loves you like a son, do you not think it about time he was told you *are* his true son?'

The others looked at each other in amazement.

'It is true,' Æthelwulf confessed shocked that Laravine was a party to such a carefully protected secret, 'Æthelred of Mercia *is* my father. My mother only told me of my true identity a few years ago.'

'Do you know why you were taken from your father?' asked Laravine.

'Because my mother is a witch...'

'I knew I had seen her before!' exclaimed Sebastian, interrupting Æthelwulf.

'Yes, *thank you* Sebastian,' Laravine said sarcastically cutting him off before he could say any more

'Sorry,' Sebastian whispered, remembering the night they had spent together in St Albans and not wanting to expand too much on what happened in front of the others.

Laravine looked back at Æthelwulf. 'You have served your father well. When you see him next, do what is right. He will thank you for it, he will need you more than ever in the not-too-distant future. Hold the charm that your mother gave you close; it will both guide you and protect you. You will need it in the fight against Tuan.'

'How do you know my mother?' asked Æthelwulf.

'Sebastian and I were in search of knights willing to join the Order of the

Brotherhood,' Laravine replied, 'and our quest led us to the lands of Mercia. It was then that we were introduced to May, your mother, almost forty years ago.'

Sebastian had the grace to blush and buried his face in his bowl before anyone noticed his discomfort.

Laravine then turned to Arnor and fixed his gaze on him. 'I have heard your father's name more than once. Uther was a man of integrity; you must be the same. I know the tragedy you carry in your heart, but do not let the murder of your wife Megan, and the child you called Mary, affect your judgement. They wait for you and, when the time is ready, they will contact you.'

'I will gladly join them when it is time,' said Arnor quietly.

'No, I believe you have already decided on a different journey to them, but for now that is all I can see. Beware of the path you choose, Arnor of Merion.'

Sebastian was next to find Laravine looking at him. 'What?' he asked. 'I have no secrets.'

'I know that,' replied Laravine, 'so do your companions. All I ask is that you do not compromise your own wellbeing. Be aware of your own limitations. Do not forget what happened when you and Falhinir first met at Dover?'

'I understand what you mean,' Sebastian replied, finishing the last of his broth and making it clear he did not want to discuss the matter any further.

'And finally, we come to you, Falhinir of Romney,' said Laravine with a sigh of relief, 'You have the most difficult choice of any of us. You have been forced to make difficult choices already and there are many more choices to make in the months to come. I can only encourage you to open your heart and help you understand your journey a little more clearly, but that is all. Ceridwen will open your eyes as to what you must do. You will have to be both strong and brave. You have already learnt much since you left your home, but beware, you will face the hardest lesson of all when you confront Tuan.'

'Do you know of my family? Are they safe?' asked Falhinir, anxious for any information Laravine had to offer.

Laravine closed his eyes and took a deep breath. 'I am not strong enough to see that far, I am sorry.' He opened his eyes and looked around the table. Everybody was pensively staring at him, wondering what he would say next. 'Please, stay here tonight, there is still much for you to see clearly before you leave these lands.'

The party agreed to stay for the night, much to the delight of Laravine, who seemed thrilled to have the company. The companions imagined that he didn't get that many passing visitors, the centre of the forest lands was as hidden from normal travellers as it was possible to be. He excused himself from the table and left to go into the forest and collect the ingredients for the evening meal. Arnor and Æthelwulf left shortly after to tend to the horses, leaving Sebastian and Falhinir alone to reflect on what they had learnt from their mysterious host.

'How do you know Laravine?' Falhinir asked his friend.

'We met an awful long time ago,' answered Sebastian, leaning back in his chair, he began to recount the strange tale of how he and Laravine had become friends; 'It was over forty years ago, in the Kingdom of Northumbria, a long way from here, ruled by King Oswald. It was the day of All Hallows' Eve and we were at the great feast within the walls of the castle. It must have been around the witching hour when the festivities were silenced by the most terrible scream that resounded throughout the castle. Running to the towers, we surveyed the surrounding lands, it was one of my men that first noticed them emerging from the darkness, coming at us from nowhere, their unearthly glow accentuated by the moonlight.'

'What did he see?' Falhinir interjected.

'They were the souls of men carried by spectral horses, their faces hidden by robes of black, they carried swords that seemed to illuminate them through the dark night.

As they came closer the very air that we breathed seemed to freeze and they brought with them a feeling of certain dread. We could only watch in terror as they charged through the gates of the castle as if they were not there. I had never seen such as sight. We ran from the tower and back into the castle where these malevolent ghosts laid waste to the entire fortress. Men were thrown across rooms and inexplicable fires ravaged the longhouses that encompassed the castle. It was amid this chaos that the doors of the great hall flung open and a tall, robed man entered. He stood in the centre of the room and looked around him. Having been trapped by a piece of falling debris, I was unable to move and could only watch as this man pulled an old staff from within his brown robes and hold it out before him. He proceeded to speak words which I had never heard before and a light began to glow from the staff. It was an awesome sight, for as he pointed the light in the direction of the spirits, they seemed to wither and vanish! Within a short time, peace was restored to the castle and the stranger introduced himself as Laravine, a shaman of the highest order who had been chasing the ghosts for some time. In thanks for his help in ridding the castle of the spirits, the King appointed him his soothsayer and gave him a home within the royal court.'

Falhinir was fascinated by the story. 'Why was he chasing the ghosts?' he asked.

'That is a tale for another time, perhaps,' said Laravine, placing the fresh ingredients upon the table, 'Sebastian, Falhinir has enough to think about without you filling his head with such tales.'

'I will tell you some other time,' Sebastian whispered to his young friend as Laravine walked into the adjoining room.

Falhinir acknowledged him with a smile. 'What do you think Laravine meant when he said we still have much to see?' he asked with a puzzled expression.

'I'm sure I don't know,' Sebastian replied sardonically, for he never really understood much of what Laravine had said. In fact, he had never really understood Laravine in all the years he had known him!

As the darkness of the cold winter evening crept among the trees, the forest began to take on a sinister form. The appearance, the sounds, and even the air were altered as the light slowly ebbed away from the woodland. The companions had ventured into the clearing from below ground but were careful to not leave the protection of the shadow of the oak.

Falhinir had gone one better and had climbed through the ancient limbs until was sitting high among the branches of the massive oak. He was reflecting upon what Laravine had told him earlier in the day and wanted to be alone for a bit. As he looked below him, he could see Sebastian, Æthelwulf and Arnor. They were all sitting separately, deep in thought. Well, except Sebastian, he was waiting for Laravine to finish cooking his dinner! That man could eat forever, thought Falhinir.

When the clearing was almost totally

dark, Sebastian decided it was time for them to go inside. He wasn't particularly fond of the cold, damp woodland. He preferred to be warm and dry. The two knights remained where they were and Sebastian stomped down the root staircase alone

From his bower Falhinir gazed up into the dark skies. The night was mostly clear with a full bright moon, its delicate rays broken by just a few light clouds. The stars were shining and plentiful. By now the dampness of the forest floor had given rise to the mist again that seemed to dance when the light, icy breeze weaved through the wood. Maybe it was the thought of the Marsh mists again but Falhinir's thoughts turned to his family, and for reasons he did not know, his mother. Though she had died when he was eight years of age, he could still remember her soft voice and the way she used to hold him. He firmly believed that at that moment she was watching over him. He fervently hoped she would continue to guide him into making the right decisions that would inevitably face them in the future.

Æthelwulf sat upright upon the damp, leafy ground. He could do nothing but think of his father, Æthelred of Mercia. The closest he had to a father when he was growing up was his uncle. He would visit when he could but being a knight, he was not home much and did not have time for a family of his own. He knew it was his mother's decision to leave Mercia, but only because it would have been harmful for the King if anyone had ever discovered he had offspring by a witch. Not to mention in times of war Æthelred's enemies would have tried to harm the child. He wanted to tell the King what his mother had disclosed but what good could come of it? He did not want to inherit the Kingdom? The constant wars had taken a heavy toll upon the people of Mercia, not least the King himself. How would King Æthelred respond to such news and the deceit of his mother? She broke the King's heart when she told him that she had to leave, what good would it do to break it again? Æthelwulf had never been so confused and in need of his mother's counsel.

Arnor was leaning against a tree, staring vacantly into the darkness of the forest. His mind wandered as he recalled his wife and child, reminiscing about how happy they were when they lived on their farm, several years before he had been forced to choose the life of a knight. As the memories played in his head, they turned to the terrible day he lost everything he held dear. The story playing in his head was interrupted by Laravine calling out to him and the others from the entrance to the oak, breaking his concentration. As he got to his feet, flinching slightly as he heard the sound of his wife fading in his memory, he could see Falhinir climbing down from the branches in the faint moonlight. Æthelwulf was re-emerging from the wood and, rather expectedly, he just caught a glimpse of Sebastian hurrying into the oak.

Not a single word was spoken as the friends sat down at the table. Laravine knew what they had all been thinking. He was feeling a little remorseful about stirring memories and emotions they would rather have forgotten, but he knew that if they were to defeat Tuan, they would have to overcome these feelings or the evil Druid could exploit their weaknesses. He knew that they had the capacity to lay the demons to rest in their pasts, but Laravine could still feel the unease he had felt earlier, he did not like it at all. Something was terribly wrong, but he was not strong enough to see what it was. He knew there was nothing he could do. *Perhaps Ceridwen will be able to uncover the reason for this awful feeling,* he thought to himself, taking a meagre sip from his bowl.

Once they had eaten, everybody helped clear away the table. When that was done Laravine stoked up the fire until it was roaring furiously, the damp wood crackling in the heat. His four guests gathered round the hearth for warmth. The winter had crept up on them and it felt like it had well and truly set in. It would not be long before the first snow would fall upon the treetops of the Forest Lands.

Sebastian did not feel entirely comfortable as his eyes wandered about Laravine's home. In the light of the fire the ancient carved faces took on a menacing appearance. He decided to move closer to the others. Nobody had said a word for over an hour and the atmosphere in the room was very sombre indeed as everyone sat alone with their thoughts.

'I think it is time I retired,' said Laravine, getting up from his seat near the fire, 'this night will hold many unsettling surprises for each of you. This forest is a sapient place, it knows the thoughts of men, learn from what you see.' And with that he went to his chamber, leaving the others beside the fire.

The four friends glanced at each other; uncertainty etched upon each of their faces in turn.

'What do you think he meant by that?' asked Sebastian worriedly.

'I don't want to know!' Arnor exclaimed.

'Why don't we just get out of here, this place is evil, I think we should get the map and leave.'

'It is too dark, said Æthelwulf, 'we will never find our way out of the forest. We will just have to try and get some sleep and wait to see what the morning brings.'

Arnor was frustrated, the situation he had found himself in was very unsettling. He did not want to be reminded of the dark places that dwelled in his memory. He decided he would get up and take a walk outside leaving the others by the fire. The three other companions thought it would be best if they tried to sleep despite their misgivings. They placed furs upon the ground around the fire and lay down upon them each making sure there was a goodly distance between him and the next man. Slowly, one by one they began to drift off into fitful slumber.

Arnor left the chamber and made his way up the root. Filled stairway. He was deep in thought as he set out to walk beyond the protective canopy of the great oak. So deep in thought was he that before he realized it, he had wandered out of the clearing and was in the midst of the forest. The mist had risen again, giving the wood a strange glow in the moonlight. As he walked silently through the trees, he could hear the unfamiliar sounds of the forest. Searching about him, he was suddenly alerted to the presence of a figure standing still in the moonlight, their features hidden in the mist. 'Falhinir, is that you?' he asked, walking towards the mysterious form.

The mysterious figure was the same height as Falhinir, but as he got closer, he could see it was the outline of a woman. Thinking it may be another of Morrigan's demons he drew his sword and cautiously approached her. He was just a short distance away when she called out to him. 'You do not need your weapon,' she said, 'the forest is protecting you this night.' Arnor was stopped in his tracks. He immediately recognised the voice, and could feel his heart beginning to race, causing him to feel a little light-headed.

'Megan?' he called. 'It cannot be, how can you be here? You are dead!' He fell to his knees. 'You are dead,' he repeated under his breath.

The woman glided over in the mist and stood before him. Arnor looked up, and to his amazement he could see that it was indeed Megan, his wife. She wiped a tear from his cheek. Arnor closed his eyes and placed his hand over hers, holding it to his face. Her skin was just how he remembered it, soft, warm and fair. Weeping, he opened his eyes and looked up at her once more. She was beautiful. Her long, dark, curly hair reached down to her shoulders. Her eyes were of the most luscious green, and the burgundy bodice she was wearing accentuated her slender figure, looking exactly the same as she did the last time he saw her alive. 'Why are you here?' he asked tearfully. 'How can you be here?'

Megan held Arnor's hand as he rose to his feet. 'My love, I am here to help you,' she said, 'I know of the choice that has been placed before you. I beg you to do what is right.'

'I intend to,' he replied, 'I will do what I must. Don't you want the same?'

'Of course, I want nothing more than to be with you, but do not put your trust in those you know to be driven by evil. There is one close to you who treads with the Devil. They will destroy you *and* your friends. This cannot be allowed to happen.'

'I know what must be done,' said Arnor, 'you need not fear.'

'But I do fear my love, I fear for you. Please, listen to what I have said. I must go.'

'Please do not leave me. Where is Mary? Is she not with you?'

When Arnor opened his eyes, he found himself alone once more, lying beneath the mighty oak tree. Confused, he stood up and looked around him. *What had I seen? Was it a dream?* He asked himself. *It seemed so real*. By now the cold air had started to creep into his bones and silently he retreated into the tree to be near the warmth of the fire and his companions.

Sometime later, Falhinir sat upright. Looking around, he could see Arnor, Æthelwulf and Sebastian in a deep slumber. Not knowing why he had woken, he shut his eyes again and tried to regain sleep, but he was too agitated and could not.

Feeling unsettled, he got up and walked over to the bowl of water sitting on a small table in the corner of the room to splash some on his face. He caught his reflection in a large mirror. Celtic in design, it was leaning against the wall behind the bowl. Falhinir screwed his eyes tightly shut as the cold water landed on his face. He licked a little from his lips as he reached for a cloth. The liquid had a peculiar salty, irony taste. He wiped his face and reopened his eyes. Falhinir could hardly breathe as he looked into bowl, for the cool, clear water Falhinir had washed his face in had turned to blood! And worse was yet to come. Falhinir dropped the blood-soaked cloth in the bowl in horror as he glanced into mirror. To his utter shock he found that he was no longer looking at his own face, but into that of his dead uncle, Asgrim, scarred and spattered with blood, just as they had found him on the barn door in Romney. Terrified, he let out an almighty scream!

In his chamber Laravine found that sleep eluded him too. He was concerned for Falhinir and the others. He shuddered as he heard Falhinir's cry from the next room, but he knew he could not interfere, no matter how distressing the manifestation.

Falhinir picked up the rag and inspected it, for the terrible vision was gone in an instant. There was only water in the bowl and on the cloth, and his reflection was once again his own. His pulse was racing as he sat down and placed his head in his hands. He lifted his head and looked over at the others. They were all still deeply asleep, none of them had so much as stirred. *Surely, they must have heard me?* Falhinir thought to himself. He picked up a log and placed it upon the dying embers of the fire, along with a little kindling. Once the fire was alive once more, Falhinir made himself comfortable upon the animal skin, and although he could not help but play the terrifying incident over and over in his mind, it wasn't long before he was once again in a deep sleep.

It was the smell of Laravine's cooking that woke his guests, Sebastian first, of course. As each of them woke, so they joined Laravine at the table.

'That was *the* best night's sleep I have had for a long time,' said Sebastian, helping himself to breakfast.

'I had a terrible night,' said Falhinir, almost sulking.

'Well, I would agree with Sebastian,' said Æthelwulf. 'What about you Arnor?'

'I don't want to talk about it!' he snapped in reply.

'How is it that Æthelwulf and I had a good sleep and you two did not?' asked Sebastian.

'The forest will only show itself to those that need to see it,' Laravine interjected, easing into his chair. 'Æthelwulf, you have made your choice about informing your father and the decision to do so will be a most rewarding one. As for Sebastian, there is nothing the forest can offer you. You know where your path will lead. I do not know what your vision meant Falhinir. And as for you Arnor, listen to her words, Megan speaks the truth.'

'I gave out a cry that could have been heard by the Celts,' said Falhinir, 'yet none of you stirred.'

Laravine looked at his young friend. 'If the forest has a message for you, it will make certain that you alone will hear it.

'You mean we were put under some kind of spell?' asked Æthelwulf.

Laravine just nodded his head.

After they had all eaten it was decided that they should be on their way. There was still much travelling to do for Laravine had disclosed the night before that he did indeed have the next portion of the map. As the four companions mounted their horses, Laravine stood watching in silence. He was very sad to see his new friends, and of course his old companion Sebastian, leave. He had a pretty good idea of the meaning behind Falhinir's vision, but he wasn't sure. Maybe it was inevitable that he would be killed in much the same way as his uncle, or perhaps his uncle just could not get through to him. As for Arnor, Laravine was concerned for him, he knew he had contemplated taking his own life before and his grief had led him to make some unwise choices when he was younger, but the decision would have to be his alone.

Laravine handed Falhinir the final part of the map. 'Take this, Falhinir of Romney, it will guide you, but beware! There is much danger between here and the mountains. I wish you a safe journey, but you know that will not be the case. Farewell my friends, I hope we do meet again in much happier times.'

Falhinir leant forward on his horse and took Laravine by the hand. 'Thank you for everything Laravine, it is with a deep sadness that we depart on our most terrible journey. I too hope that we do meet again.'

'Goody bye old friend,' said Sebastian, placing his hand on Laravine's shoulder.

Arnor and Æthelwulf acknowledged their new friend with a simple nod, and with that the group slowly followed the path out of the forest that Laravine once more laid for them.

A single tear fell from Laravine's eye as he watched the four riders disappear into the thick of the woodland. He was sad that such a heavy burden had been placed on Falhinir's young shoulders as they disappeared once more back into the densely wooded forest.

Printed in Great Britain
by Amazon

59601608R00173